First Loser

CHARITY PARKERSON

Copyright

--Warning: This book is intended for readers over the age of 18.

Editor: Vicky Reese

ISBN: 978-1-946099-58-7

Contents

Introduction

SAME SITUATION. DIFFERENT MAN. *It's a beautiful mess.*

After falling for a male escort, and losing him through his own stupidity, Henry meets Tanner. Tanner is tall, dark, and handsome. He's also young, wealthy, and doesn't need Henry at all. But Henry is right back in the same boat he's been in for years, paying someone half his age to spend time with him. Even though Tanner keeps refunding his money, Henry can't let himself believe Tanner wants him for real. His mistrust is making him miserable, but Henry doesn't know how to stop.

As one owner of Cubs for Rent—a company that rents men for dates, repairmen, or simply for company, Tanner doesn't need anyone to take care of him. When he met Henry, Tanner's only intention had been to get the man out of his friend's hair. Then, Henry kept calling and booking time with Tanner. Tanner kept accepting and feelings he didn't want grew. Henry is sweet and insecure. He's gentle and awkward. Henry is everything that Tanner finds irresistible. It's too bad Henry is also too blind to see Tanner's interest as real, because Tanner is tired of trying to convince him.

FIRST LOSER

When Tanner pulls away and meets someone his age, Henry will have to come out of his shell and step up his game. Hopefully, he's not too late.

Chapter One

THE BALLROOM WAS AS bright as daylight and Tanner was equally well lit. It was the opening night of Cubs for Rent—the company Tanner had started with his brothers, Toby and Tucker. They had thrown this opening ball in their home in hopes of one day becoming the largest provider of men for rent. They wanted to seem welcoming and inclusive. In the meantime, Tanner was tired of being swarmed by vultures. He had smiled and flirted for hours, hoping to tempt as many men as possible into checking out their list of services. Now, he really wanted some peace and quiet. This wasn't his scene. He wasn't the carefree guy he had been forced to portray all night. In truth, Tanner enjoyed silence. All he wanted out of life was peace.

The band played a slow song that had men searching for partners. It had Tanner hunting an escape from the overheated ballroom and even more heated glances being tossed his way. He couldn't charm another soul. His gaze landed on his friend and mentor, Legend. Legend was the opposite of Tanner in every way. He fit in at every gathering, gave back the flirting as hard as it came his way, and he simply looked the part of the perfect escort. Blond, tall, tan, and blue-eyed, Legend was fucking perfect. Of course, tonight, the man they had hired to launch their new company looked uncomfortable as hell with some dude crowding his space. Tanner knew Legend could hold his own, but the guy trying to talk to him definitely needed saving. Legend would eat his heart for breakfast.

Henry Krill was obviously enthralled by Legend's beauty. Tanner couldn't blame the guy, but still. Even if Tanner couldn't see it written all over the guy's face, Tanner had heard the story of Henry's recently botched marriage proposal to Legend. Everyone here had likely heard the story. Legend had once worked as Henry's escort. Henry had fallen in love and asked Legend to marry him. It hadn't gone well. Legend wasn't free to be with Henry. Likely, Henry didn't know that. Escorts were in the business of making money. Not building relationships. Henry cornering Legend tonight could only end one way—with Henry getting his feelings crushed with a room full of witnesses looking on. In truth he looked too tiny to handle such a huge blow.

Without a real plan, Tanner swooped in. He snagged Henry's waist and swept him onto the dance floor without missing a step. "Let's dance."

Sweet brown eyes flashed with irritation as they locked on Tanner. Tanner's heart twisted at the sight. Henry looked way too nice for anyone at this party. "I don't want to dance."

Tanner fought a smile at Henry's petulant tone. "You're in for a real treat, then," Tanner said, pulling him closer. "I don't either."

"I was in the middle of an important discussion," Henry said, half-heartedly trying to break Tanner's hold.

Tanner tightened his grip and sailed with Henry out a side door and into the night air. Still, once they were out of the view of prying eyes, Tanner didn't release his hold. He lightly stroked the small of Henry's back. Henry looked sad. Tanner couldn't stop himself. "Trust me. I just saved you from getting your heart publicly demolished. Legend is in love with someone else." Tanner hated to be the bearer of bad news, but he also couldn't stand to see anyone humiliated with hundreds of witnesses. He knew all about feeling helpless with no one to save him.

Tanner felt the fight drain from Henry. His gaze slid away. His defeat punched Tanner in the chest.

"Oh." He stepped out of Tanner's hold. Tanner let him go. "I suppose part of me knew that. I definitely had it coming." Henry cleared his throat. He still wasn't meeting Tanner's stare. In a nervous motion, Henry tugged at his jacket. "Um. Thank you, I guess."

"I'm sorry it was necessary."

A sad smile touched Henry's lips. He visibly fought to keep it from slipping away. Tanner couldn't help but notice how handsome Henry was. He was distinguished. It was obvious he had been raised with money. There was no real way to guess his age. If Legend hadn't already been in love with someone else, Tanner could see them as a beautiful couple. Everyone would be jealous, including Tanner.

"You're one of the hosts tonight, right?"

Tanner dipped his chin. "That's right."

"I guess I should let you get back to your guests."

That was the last thing Tanner wanted. "It's fine. I don't care for crowds or dancing. Everything about this event has me mentally exhausted."

Henry finally focused on him. Tanner felt the power of Henry's attention all the way to his core. "Apologies. I don't recall your name."

"Tanner Kodiak."

Henry's eyebrows rose. "Are you any relation to Teddy Kodiak?"

A smile that felt bitter even to him touched Tanner's lips. "He's my father."

Henry's eyebrows rose. "Didn't he..."

Yeah. Tanner knew what Henry realized too late. His dad had been nuts. Pretty famously completely batshit and he had taken his kids along for the ride. After a massively successful career in baseball, and years of drug abuse, Tanner's mom passed, and Teddy snapped. He grabbed his three small children and headed for the hills. They went from lavish lifestyles to living off the land as unwilling survivalists. No one but Toby, Tanner, and Tucker knew what went down in those woods. They had endured over ten years of hell before their father took his own life. Thankfully, all his money had been in trust and they had outlived him. But they weren't normal. Not a single one of them came out of those woods untouched. They were hard on the inside—survivalist to the core. Nothing Henry chose to say could touch the truth, and as long as the triplets lived, no one would ever know the real story.

Tanner didn't force Henry to keep searching for a way to recover the conversation. "He passed when I was eighteen."

Open relief poured through Henry's features at the rescue. "I thought I'd heard that." He glanced around, visibly uncomfortable. Tanner almost left him alone to spare him. Then, Henry focused on him again. Resolve etched his face. "Since you don't like dancing or crowds, you should stay out here... with me."

There was a hint of fear in Henry's eyes. He had put himself out there with the offer. Tanner could practically feel Henry bracing for Tanner's refusal—as if everyone rejected him. Unexpected hunger washed over him. Something about weakness drove Tanner wild. He thought—maybe—it was the surge of power that went through him when he realized he could fill the emptiness. He could be the person Henry wasn't expecting to meet tonight. "Or you could come upstairs with me instead."

For what felt like forever, Henry stared at him with shock keeping his features blanked. He visibly swallowed. "Okay."

Although that was the last answer Tanner expected, he wasn't taking his offer back. He likely wouldn't see Henry again after tonight. Tanner tried not to look at things too closely. He was in a bad head-space tonight. This party had brought out the worst in him. Henry looked like a man who didn't want to be alone. Tanner didn't either. Sometimes, the company of one person who understood was all anyone needed. Maybe they both needed someone to save them tonight.

As Tanner weaved his way through the crowd, Henry stuck close to his back. Several men stopped Tanner along the way, openly flirting. The first few times, Henry stood silently waiting with his mind trapped in an internal freak out. He was fully aware he had agreed to go upstairs with a stranger because he didn't want to be alone. In a detached sort of way, he recognized Tanner was gorgeous. It wasn't until he stopped for the fifth time, so some guy could spend a second basking in Tanner's attention, that Henry really took a minute to stare at Tanner. He was big—wide shouldered and tall. His dark hair was perfectly styled, and deep dimples showed every time he flashed his perfect smile. Tanner's forest green eyes looked kind as he focused his full attention on each person who stopped him. A hint of pride worked its way into Henry's chest. Tanner had invited him upstairs. Soon, that focus would be completely on him.

Without warning, a smile tugged at the corners of Henry's mouth. Maybe life didn't suck as much as he thought. It was possible he would survive losing Legend. Another person stopped

Tanner. Tanner's gaze slid his way for half a heartbeat before focusing on the latest interruption. In that brief moment, Henry felt his desperation. He hadn't been exaggerating outside. This was sucking the life from him. Henry had been raised to be cold and cutting. Being rich enough to be rude was his superpower.

Henry set his hand on the small of Tanner's back and cut in. "Excuse us. Tanner and I need to discuss some business."

There was no one who didn't know Henry and his reach. The man who had been speaking to Tanner, immediately backed up a step. "Of course. I'll be around," he said, directing his words Tanner's way.

Tanner smiled, nodded, and promised to find him soon.

Henry steered Tanner toward the stairs, silently admonishing anyone who tried stepping into their path. In no time, they were ascending the steps in peace. The moment they were alone in the upstairs hallway, Tanner glanced his way.

"Thank you for the rescue. I realize it's ridiculous, considering the line of work I'm entering, but I've been extremely uncomfortable tonight."

Henry met his gaze. "You don't have to explain. If you feel uncomfortable, even if it's your job, you need to walk away. Your soul isn't for sale. Only your time and only on your terms."

Tanner didn't respond until they reached a closed door. When he finally spoke, he didn't look Henry's way. "I can see why Legend cared for you."

Henry couldn't look away. The flirt from downstairs was gone. This serious version of Tanner was real. Better. "You look exhausted."

A smile popped to Tanner's lips, but he didn't respond. Instead, he led Henry inside what had to be his bedroom. It was cozy. Big bed. Large, cushy chair in the corner. A door led to a bathroom. He could see a huge tub through the open doorway. It was a large room with lots of furniture, including a desk. Henry got the feeling Tanner stayed in his bedroom quite a bit. This was a gorgeous house. Even shared by three men, it had to be insanely expensive. The location, right on the edge of Lake Travis was a prime spot. Henry's curiosity spiked.

"What made you decide to start Cubs for Rent? You don't look as if you need the money."

"We don't," Tanner said, peeling off his jacket and toeing off his shoes. "The last ten years of Dad's life, he never spent a dime, and everything he had grew in investments. When he died, and everything came to us, we were set for life. Considering we haven't gone crazy spending and we've lived together for the past ten years, everything has continued growing." Tanner kept talking while unbuttoning his shirt. Henry couldn't look away. Tanner had every ounce of his focus. "In the scene here, we've met a lot of men who sell their time, for whatever reason. All legal and above reproach, of course. But we've also heard the same horror stories a million times—men stalking them, threatening them, blackmail, and every horror in between. It's really not safe. The problem is, it's all a lot of these guys know, and one of the biggest reasons they fall victim to these things is because there's no one backing them—physically or financially. They have no out. Toby, Tucker, and I sat down one day and started coming up with this plan to help while also giving ourselves something to do. We called up Legend to get his expert advice and he was pretty honest with us. No one would split their fees with us for something we weren't willing to do ourselves." Tanner shrugged. "Here we are, starting from the bottom. Once we're established, we'll keep our guys safe, but likely from the sidelines."

Henry perched on the edge of the chair and watched Tanner with fascination.

He wanted to help people. That was sweet, especially since Tanner looked miserable being the center of attention. "I'd like to be your first customer. May I hire you for the rest of the night?"

Tanner froze in the middle of taking off his belt. "I don't have sex for money."

"That's not my intention," Henry rushed to explain before he ruined things, which—honestly—he was damned good at doing. "No sex. I want you to get some sleep. Maybe eat a proper meal first, because I doubt you got one today with all this going on."

"You want to hire me to take care of me." Tanner sounded confused as he summed up Henry's offer.

"Yes."

"Why?"

21

Henry snorted at Tanner's question. "Did Legend not tell you that you should never question why someone hires you?"

The corner of Tanner's mouth lifted in a smirk. "Possibly." Tanner shook his head and sighed. "You can hire me *if* you agree to eat with me *and* you have to cuddle with me while *we* sleep."

"Deal."

It was odd. Henry had flown all the way from California only to lose the man he had shown up to win tonight, but he knew he would survive. Tanner thought Henry wanted to take care of him, but really this was self-care. He was saving himself. When Tanner fell asleep, Henry would sneak away and leave him to rest. Then, they would be even. A night of peace for the unexpected friendship

Tanner had given him in his moment of need. Maybe tonight would be the first of many.

Chapter Two

HENRY: *MAY I HIRE you for the weekend?*

Tanner: *I'll always be free for you.*

Henry: *Great. I think you need to be spoiled with a nice dinner and lots of peace.*

Tanner: *You want to hire me to take care of me again?*

Henry: *You returned my last fee. I feel moved to do a better job of bringing you comfort this time.*

Tanner: *I refunded your money because I didn't do anything to earn it.*

Henry: *It made me happy to watch the stress bleed from your shoulders. I'd pay a lot to watch it happen again.*

Tanner: *Then I guess I will see you on Friday.*

Henry: *Yes. Friday.*

Henry: *An email from my bank informs me I just received a refund from you. What's that about?*

Tanner: *I don't have sex for money.*

Henry: *Yeah, well. I didn't plan that.*

Tanner: *I know.*

Henry: *You should still keep part of the money. We didn't have sex the whole time.*

Tanner: *Shame. I'll try harder next time.*

Henry: *So, weird thought. If I plan to see you often, and I do, I think I might buy a place there. I don't like hotels and there's a cozy cabin for sale not that far from you. What do you think?*

Tanner: *The walls in hotels are regrettably thin.*

Henry: *Seriously, I swear I'm not out to seduce you. I don't know how it keeps going there.*

FIRST LOSER

Tanner: *LOL! I'm trying to seduce you. There. Do you feel better now? Buy the cabin.*

Henry: *Let me hire you for this weekend then. Go check out the place with me.*

Tanner: *Like I've said, I'm always free for you.*

Henry: *Meet me at the cabin at seven? Fee has already been paid.*

Tanner: *I'm on my way.*

Henry: *I think I pulled a muscle in my back and you still refunded my money.*

Tanner: *Poor angel. All the more reason for you to get a refund. You did most the work.*

Henry: *See me this weekend. I'll pay you double if you work this kink out of my back.*

Tanner: *Just let me know what time you'll be here and I'm your man.*

Henry: *That has a nice ring to it.*

Tanner: *It really does.*

FIRST LOSER

Austin, Texas was a lot prettier than Henry imagined before he started visiting here six months ago, or maybe the place was growing on him. The view of Lake Travis from his small cabin was amazing. Henry wished it brought him peace. Nothing did. This place came close, though. That was why he kept coming back. Sort of. Back home, in California, Henry still saw Legend's face everywhere. Quite literally since Legend married into one of the richest families in the world. That meant Legend attended all the same events, ran in the same circles, and had the life Henry had hoped to give him once upon a time. Anytime Legend's sexy blue gaze moved his way, it was like Henry was a stranger now. Legend never acknowl-edged him at all. It was Henry's fault. He was the one who fucked up. It was a hard pill to swallow. At one time, he had hon-estly considered Legend his best friend. The time they spent together was the only true companionship he had in his life. How depressing. He'd paid for the service.

As sad as it was for him to confess, at fifty-two Henry still hadn't truly lived. For many years he had been held back by convention. In his glory days, men like him had to keep their sexuality hid-den. While he had several secret ren-dezvous with beautiful men, Henry had never been given the privilege of show-ing one off to the world as his. That was also thanks in part to his shitty family. Then, one day, he had woken up old and the moment was lost. He had thought his chance was gone.

Then, two years ago, Henry met a male escort—Legend. It was such a fitting name. Unlike most escorts, Legend went by his real name. He chose his clients and never messed with anyone who didn't treat him like he deserved. Legend was genuine and sweet. Henry found himself searching for more and more reasons to hire him. He always chose weekend long events so he could have as much of Legend as possible. Sometimes, he even traveled out of state to events just to have a reason for Legend to be there. The closer he got to Legend, the harder it became to be around him, because Legend owned his heart. Henry knew it was stupid. He shouldn't have let things get so far. It was Legend. He was everything Henry wished he could have and felt he missed when he was young enough to have him.

Then, the oddest thing happened, Henry heard himself asking to marry Legend. Once the offer was out there, Henry knew they were at a crossroads. Either Legend would accept, and Henry would have to deal with knowing Legend only wanted his money, or Legend would decline, and Henry would never see him again. Unfortunately, he was one hundred percent certain he was making all the same mistakes with someone new. Because Henry could not stay away from Tanner. He had tried. Between every visit, he told himself he wouldn't return to this town. He would not humiliate himself again the way he had with Legend. Henry never lasted more than two weeks without Tanner.

The man ruled his every thought. Henry had gone farther to make Tanner his than he had ever dreamed of going for Legend. In truth, Tanner scared the hell out of him. Henry didn't know how to stop. He very much feared there was no line he wouldn't cross.

Warm lips brushed his nape. Henry's eyes fell closed. He sucked in a breath as his body immediately responded. Henry would know Tanner's lips in the dark and surrounded by a thousand other people. A single red rose appeared in front of him. Henry's heart skipped a beat. "You're regretting me again. I can practically taste it." Tanner's arms encircled him. Henry found himself cradled against the world's sexiest chest as he brought the rose to his nose. Still, Henry didn't tear his gaze from the view through his French doors.

"No." Henry wasn't sure it wasn't a lie.

Tanner brushed a kiss across the shell of his ear. "It's okay. I can go."

Henry found the strength to turn. Forest green eyes met him. They were filled with understanding and a hint of hurt. Tanner was so big and comfy. He was nice and sexy. He was also half Henry's age and wouldn't be here if Henry hadn't hired him. Self-hatred swelled his throat. Tanner confused him. Henry no longer had the strength to save himself. He didn't know why he couldn't meet someone through normal means.

"You returned my last fee again."

A smirk touched Tanner's lips. He undid Henry's tie and popped the top button on Henry's shirt. "If I have my way, you'll get your fee back for today too." He kept unbuttoning Henry's shirt without an ounce of shame. "I've told you I don't have sex for money." Tanner paused. "Unless you don't want me."

Panic rose in Henry's chest. Tanner couldn't leave. "You know I do."

Tanner shuffled closer. Desire owned Henry. "Do you? I'm not so sure today."

Tanner always made him brave. He never expected to have someone so incredibly sexy want him. There was no doubt that he did. The flush on Tanner's cheeks and the erection poking Henry couldn't be faked. Henry's fingers went to the button on Tanner's jeans. He popped the button and slid Tanner's zipper down. "Are you still doubting me? I didn't come thirteen hundred miles for anyone else." He dipped his head and kissed Tanner's collarbone. "I'm here for you."

A sexy rumble of laughter vibrated from Tanner's chest. "I guess you're taking your money back then."

Goddamn. Henry didn't know what to think. He didn't understand why Tanner kept returning his money. The man didn't try to see him if Henry didn't hire him, yet he always refunded any fees Henry paid. Henry thought he had been confused while falling for Legend. Falling for Tanner was so much worse. There were no clear lines. Legend had always been a professional before Henry wiped away those lines. Tanner never tried to be professional. He never pretended to be working. It was as if they were a couple, except they weren't, and it was hell. Tanner owned all of Henry's thoughts. He woke in the middle of the night when they weren't together, burning for Tanner. It was odd how willing he had been to marry Legend, yet what he felt for Tanner eclipsed everything, and Henry didn't know how to give him an inch. That realization had Henry slipping to his knees and leaving the rose on the floor.

The sound Tanner made as Henry circled his crown with his tongue made the muscles in Henry's stomach contract. For a full minute, he couldn't do anything but try to drag that noise from Tanner again. Henry wanted it. His gaze flipped upward. Tanner stared down at him with flushed cheeks and crazed eyes. Pride swelled Henry's chest. He took Tanner down his throat. Tanner growled—like a wild animal. In that moment, Henry would have done anything for Tanner. He was that desperate to own him.

Tanner snagged his arms and urged him to his feet. Henry nearly whimpered at the loss of Tanner's cock. Tanner shushed him, making Henry wonder if he had made the noise after all. "I love your mouth." Tanner chuckled. It was a soft and sexy rumble. "A little too much. I want to come inside you while you're straddling my hips."

Henry couldn't argue with the picture Tanner painted. He let Tanner lead him to the bedroom. Henry stood still while Tanner stripped away the last of their clothing. There was something hypnotizing about Tanner. He made Henry useless. When Tanner wasn't around, Henry had tons of fantasies about taking control, bringing this huge cub to his knees. It never happened in reality. The second they were together, Henry was always enslaved.

Tanner sat on the edge of the bed. Henry stood entranced by the vision Tanner presented while rolling on a condom and oiling up the sheath. Tanner's gaze met his. Henry's heartbeat pounded in his ears. Tanner's hands found Henry's ass. He lured Henry closer, holding Henry's stare as he urged Henry to straddle his lap. Each breath came harder than the last. Henry braced his hands on Tanner's wide shoulders. Tanner's gorgeous green gaze held him hostage. Henry's breath left him on a gasp as Tanner fingered his hole, stretching him and making room for a larger intrusion.

"You're so gorgeous," Tanner said, sounding sincere and turned on. "I think about having you like this non-stop. You have no idea how much I crave the way you're looking at me right now—like no other men exist. Like I'm it for you."

The desire to say Tanner was it for him rose in Henry's throat until he thought he might choke on the confession. Tanner's huge cock filled Henry's ass. The ability to think or speak left Henry. All he could do was feel. Tanner fell backward, as if surrendering, and giving Henry the freedom to do whatever he wanted to Tanner's body. His gaze moved over the huge expanse of hairy chest. Henry's cock leaked. He couldn't stop himself from moving, riding Tanner, and using him to get off. Henry didn't hesitate to find the perfect angle. The way Tanner watched him through half-closed lids and with parted lips drove Henry. As Henry set a pace to please, Tanner lightly stroked Henry's cock, making him crazy.

"That's it, baby," Tanner said, praising him. "Ride me. Take what you want." His touch firmed until Henry was torn between fucking his palm and taking Tanner's dick as hard as possible. He wanted everything. "Mhmm. I want your cum on my skin. Drown me in it, sexy." Between Tanner's words and the vision he presented, Henry was right on the edge. Tanner stroked faster. Henry held his breath and thrust against Tanner's palm while taking his dick. Everything slowed. It was like time stopped and took a breath before ecstasy washed over Henry. His body shook from the power of the orgasm rolling over him. He was useless. Tanner rolled, pinning Henry beneath his huge body. He turned wild, using Henry's body. Cries clogged Henry's throat as Tanner slammed inside him. Henry gasped open mouthed, trying to drag air into his lungs while Tanner pounded that internal button that made Henry a mess. Words left him. Henry had no clue what he said. He imagined he begged for the abuse. Harder. Faster. More. It would never be enough. Even if Tanner spent the next fifty years fucking him, it wouldn't be enough to satisfy Henry's heart. Henry was screwed—literally and figuratively. He wanted this man. This one. No other person would ever be enough, and Henry had no idea where to go with that. He had no idea how to win him.

FIRST LOSER

Tanner couldn't stop stealing tastes of Henry's skin. Henry had bought this cabin six months ago, not long after their first night together. He kept coming back and Tanner couldn't stay away. The more time Tanner spent with Henry, the more he wanted. Tanner couldn't explain what happened the first night they fell into bed together. They had been in Tanner's room, talking about Henry's plans for the evening. Henry had looked at Tanner, and said, "You're such an amazing person." Then, Henry had blushed like he couldn't believe he had said the words out loud. Hunger like Tanner had never experienced had washed over him in that moment. To be honest, he had somewhat fallen on

Henry like a starving man, ripping away his clothes and biting at his skin. Henry had given it back every bit as desperately. In that moment, Tanner knew he had connected with a soul every bit as lonely as him. Tanner had been incapable of staying away ever since. They had something beautiful. Something real. He needed more. Tanner didn't know what it was about the man. He just made Tanner feel powerful and irresistible, yet comforted. Since Tanner hadn't felt cared for or comfortable anywhere since he was seven, Henry was like crack for Tanner. There was no chance he could quit him.

Since starting Cubs for Rent, Tanner had been hired for dozens of odd reasons—dates for events, a dinner with one girl's family so they wouldn't know she preferred women, and the occasional home repair or heavy lifting job. In every case, Tanner had known the exact place to draw the line. There were no lines with Henry. While sometimes they talked for hours first, they always ended up here. In this bed. They had an intense connection Tanner didn't understand. The one thing he knew was he didn't want to be with anyone else.

Tanner kissed the corner of Henry's mouth. A hum rose in his throat. The desire to keep Henry with him forever—to show him off to the world—was overwhelming him. "You should let me take you to dinner. I want to make everyone jealous."

"I'd love to go to dinner with you, if you'll let me pay you for your time. I don't feel right spending time with you for free."

Tanner froze. A self-deprecating smile tugged at Tanner's lips. Every time. Every fucking time, Tanner let Henry suck him in. He shook his head. The fake smile he wore grew becoming a derisive snort. This was the other thing he knew about his so-called relationship with Henry. Tanner was alone in his feelings. While Henry obviously enjoyed fucking Tanner, that was where things ended for Henry. Tanner meant nothing to him. Tanner didn't know how to stop being the whore.

"What?"

At Henry's question, Tanner focused on him. He took a breath. This moment had been six months in the making. "All right, but maybe don't hire me anymore after tonight."

Henry blinked, looking like Tanner slapped him. He cleared his throat, visibly trying to temper his reaction. "Can I ask why?"

Tanner pursed his lips, fighting against himself. He didn't want this. He didn't want to lose Henry, but he also couldn't make Henry want him. Tanner slipped from the bed and gathered his clothes. He didn't focus on Henry again until he was dressed and positive of his own mind. "I've been returning your money for over six months. If you haven't figured out why by now, you won't ever. It's long past the time I should accept that and find someone who wants me."

Henry's expression transformed from confused to irritated. "Are you really trying to claim that you want more with me? If I didn't hire you, I wouldn't get to see you at all. You don't call or text unless it's to discuss me hiring you for the weekend. You don't have anything to do with me beyond that if I'm not here. I hire you and you show up. Other than refunding my money, you're not exactly fighting to be with me."

Tanner didn't want to fight. It was possible he had a touch of PTSD from his father's constant anger. He couldn't tolerate yelling or that feeling in his gut when someone was angry with him. Henry spoiling for a fight had him wanting to apologize to keep the peace, but he couldn't cheat himself any longer with Henry. He took a breath. "I'm sorry." Fuck. He always ended up apologizing. A sad smile touched his lips. He softened his voice. "You don't want me, baby. If I called or texted between visits, you would never come here. Only the fact that you haven't heard from me keeps you hiring me. I don't know if you're ashamed of me for some reason. Or hell, maybe the idea of dating anyone exclusively is distasteful to you. No matter the reason, I can't let you keep trying to buy me so you can keep walking away guilt free."

"That's not—"

Tanner made a slashing motion, cutting Henry off before things got heated. He held Henry's stare, hoping he would see Tanner's honesty. "I want to be with you." Tanner needed Henry to see him and believe him. "For me, being with you is real and could be amazing. But I can't make you feel what you don't, and if you felt anything for me, you wouldn't be trying to pay me right now."

Henry made a helpless gesture. "I bought this cabin to be near you. Why would I do that if I didn't care about you?"

It took every ounce of Tanner's self-control not to roll his eyes. "Did you? Or did you buy this place so you could hide me from society? After all, if Legend doesn't know about me, then you'll still be free if his marriage doesn't work out, and he decides to come back."

For the first time ever, Tanner seemed to hit a nerve. Henry's face hardened. "This has nothing to do with Legend. We," he said motioning between them. "have nothing to do with Legend."

Tanner bit back a growl. "This has everything to do with him. I'm tired of keeping you company while you wait for him. I sick of being your second choice."

"You're not."

A wave of sadness washed over Tanner. He shook his head, fighting back the depression that always threatened to overwhelm him. For a moment, he stared at Henry, wishing every word was true, but it wasn't, and he couldn't pretend any longer. "Fine. I guess I'm just the first loser then."

Exasperation etched every line of Henry's body. "That's just saying the same thing in a different way."

"Exactly." Tanner walked away before he slipped back into the dark place he had been before tons of counseling and Henry came along. Maybe he had some daddy issues and that kept him clinging to the first older man who treated him kindly. It's not like he would know. That didn't mean he had to let another older man destroy his peace again. Sometimes he had to choose—his heart or his mind. In the end, it was much easier for him to deal with a broken heart. He might not survive another broken mind.

Chapter Three

TANNER: *WHAT DO YOU have going on tonight?*

Tucker: *I'm working the door at Howling Twister.*

Tanner: *?? How did that happen?*

Tucker: *I volunteered. They're donating all their profits tonight to that friend of Toby's who had that bad wreck. To pull it off, they needed volunteers.*

Tanner. *Oh. That's awesome. I might stop by.*

Tucker: *I'll be here.*

Henry: *I'm sorry. May I please see you tonight?*

Tanner: *Can't. Howling Twister is donating tonight's profits to my brother's friend who was in a wreck. I said I'd go.*

Henry: *Just five minutes. That's all I need.*

Henry: *I take your lack of response as a no.*

Tanner: *I was in the shower, but you've had lots of time to figure things out. I'm sorry. Truly, I am. But you don't want me, not really, and I'm tired of waiting to be graced with scraps of your time. Maybe I don't really know my worth, but you sure as hell don't either.*

The parking lot of Howling Twister bar was slammed. Tanner hoped that meant lots of money being raised. He couldn't imagine being in Toby's friend's shoes. Loyal had gone from an active lifestyle to trapped in a wheelchair overnight. It all sounded like a nightmare to him. Toby and Loyal hadn't talked in a while—for good reason, but if Tanner and his brothers knew nothing else, they understood feeling helpless. Tanner wasn't surprised Toby and Tucker were volunteering their time. If Tanner hadn't been so focused on someone who didn't even want him, Tanner might have been around to find some way to help too.

Tanner spotted Tucker right away. He was surrounded by people, checking IDs before letting anyone inside. Tucker stood nearly a foot taller than everyone else. He was huge and hard to miss. Since they were the same height, Tucker spotted him at the same time. He nodded and urged people aside so Tanner could join him at the door.

"Hey. I thought you had a weekend-long job?"

Tanner nodded. His gaze swept the crowd. He couldn't look Tucker in the eye while admitting he had been used... again. "I did too. Looks like I'm free."

Since Tucker was a good person, he didn't hand Tanner the I-told-you-so he deserved. Tucker had been warning Tanner against Henry every step of the way, telling him Henry was only using him. He was a rich man's toy. It would have served Tanner right for Tucker to gloat. He didn't. "That's too bad. But hey, I'm glad you're here. Can you do this for me for a minute while I run inside?" He laughed. "I'm about to piss all over myself."

Tanner tried not to blanch. He didn't know shit about working the door of a nightclub. "Sure. I just check IDs, right?"

Tucker rolled his eyes. "You've got this, dude. Two minutes."

With a nod, Tanner slid into Tucker's spot and started checking dates. It took him a second to calculate birth years and ensure he wasn't letting anyone under eighteen inside. Ten or fifteen people into his new gig, he had things moving right along. He was a little proud of how professional he seemed. Then a driver's license appeared beneath his nose. There was a hot pink post-it note stuck to the ID.

Please say I'm banned so I can go home.

A snort escaped Tanner before he could call it back. He quickly smothered the sound. Tanner looked up and into the lightest eyes he had ever seen. They were almost otherworldly. His mouth went dry.

"Step to the side, please," Tanner said, motioning the man to the side. He kept a hold on the man's driver's license as he waved the rest of the group inside. "The rest of you, go ahead."

One young blond man lingered, but a stern look from Tanner got him moving. Once the guy was free from his friends, Tanner glanced down at his license again. "So, Orion Moon." Tanner smiled at the name. The dude definitely had free-spirited parents. He passed Orion's ID back. "You're officially free of your friends." He eyed Orion from head to toe. The guy was skinny and dressed like he gave no fucks. His jeans were baggy, and one leg of his pants was tucked into the top of his work boot, but there was something a little adorable about him. "Unless I can convince you to stay for me, that is."

Orion looked confused. "Why?"

"Why what?"

"Why would you want me to stay for you?" Orion sounded damn pragmatic and not the least bit interested.

It was Tanner's turn to be confused. "Because I think you're hot. Why are you in such a rush to go home? You obviously have friends who want to spend time with you."

Orion shifted from one foot to the other and rubbed his arm. "Those aren't my friends. We work together. Also... I got a new book today."

"A book," Tanner repeated, wondering if he had heard that right. At Orion's disgruntled expression, Tanner decided to run with it. "What's it about?"

Orion's gaze shot from side to side, as if he thought to run. "Um, bears."

Tanner checked a few more IDs while keeping up his end. "Bears." Tanner didn't know why he couldn't stop repeating everything. "The animals or the hairy dudes?"

To Tanner's surprise, Orion focused on him without an ounce of artifice. His gaze didn't move. Orion's eyes were gorgeous. Tanner couldn't look away. "Both, actually. Bear shifters."

This was such an odd conversation. Tanner couldn't stop. "Do you—"

"Kodiak."

Tanner turned his head at the sound of his last name. He tossed a wave at the guy in line who had called out. They went to the same gym. Like everyone else who couldn't tell his brothers and him apart, the guy had fallen back on Tanner's last name.

Tucker reappeared, setting him free. "Whew. Thanks, bro. I might survive now. I'll take over."

"Cool. I'm going to…" he turned his head. Orion was gone. Tanner scanned the crowd. He caught a glimpse of Orion's retreating form, weaving his way through the parking lot. Without a backward look or explanation, Tanner took off after him. "Orion, hold up."

Orion's shoulders visibly fell. Tanner suppressed a laugh as Orion turned, looking defeated. "Did you need something else?"

"Yeah. Your number."

Orion's expression never changed. He wasn't the least bit tempted in any way. It was written all over his face. Honestly, it was refreshing. No one felt like a friend since he started Cubs for Rent.

62

Everyone wanted something. All Tanner wanted was Henry and that wasn't going to happen. Orion was a nice distraction.

"Why would you want my number?"

Tanner shook his head. "Jesus. It's like you've never been hit on before."

Something unnamed passed over Orion's features and disappeared as quickly. "People don't flirt with me."

"I call bullshit."

Orion didn't smile. "People don't ask for my number."

"I just did."

A line appeared between Orion's brows. "What are you after?"

Tanner didn't back down. "Let's go do something."

"I want to go home," Orion said, refusing to give an inch.

He didn't know Tanner. Tanner didn't quit. "Then take me with you. If I annoy you, you can put me out on the side of the road."

For a moment, Orion stared at him with zero emotion. Finally, his chin dipped slightly. "Fine, but just so you know, I own a gun."

Tanner shrugged. "It's Texas. One was assigned to you at birth."

Instead of laughing, as Tanner hoped, Orion gave him a sharp nod and turned away. Tanner raced to catch up. Maybe he was looking for a distraction from his breaking heart, but Tanner knew a good deal when he saw one. If nothing else, at least he wouldn't be alone tonight with his thoughts. That was something.

FIRST LOSER

Howling Twister turned out to be a bar that was swarming with people. For several minutes, Henry sat in his rental car and stared at the front door. His chest hurt. He had come to Texas for the weekend, fully intent on spending time with the only person he cared about. Now everything was a wreck and he didn't even understand what happened. One second, they had been kissing and the next Tanner was done. They had never truly fought about the money aspect of things. Henry paid and Tanner returned it. That was the end of things. Henry never suspected that Tanner harbored so much resentment over that.

He wanted to apologize. Talk things through. Henry didn't know where to start. He only knew he had to try. Tanner had said they were real. He had stunned Henry with that one, and then walked away. Henry had to fix it.

A bar was bit intimidating, especially this one. The place looked like a backwoods honkytonk where people came to drink bad beer and line dance. Henry didn't fit the scene. He didn't know if he could storm a place filled with people in their twenties and scream his feelings over the loud music drifting all the way out to his car. That wasn't the only fear keeping him glued to his seat. Tanner stood with one of his brothers at the front entrance already surrounded by a ton of men. It was funny that Henry knew which of the identical men was Tanner. They held themselves differently. There was always a hint of melancholy in every move Tanner made. His entire demeanor was darker than his brother. Part of that was Henry's doing. The rest... Henry didn't know what caused Tanner's solemn nature. All he knew was, he wanted to fix it. The problem was, Henry wasn't brave. He never had been. Henry came from an overbearing family that had always demanded perfection. He was supposed to be quiet and never embarrass his name. No one taught him to stand up and stand out. He didn't know how to follow his heart. But he had to start somewhere, because he couldn't lose Tanner.

As Henry looked on, Tanner darted from the door. Henry watched with his heart in his throat as Tanner spoke with a skinny guy who couldn't have been more than eighteen. He recognized Tanner's smile. It was the flirtatious one he usually reserved only for Henry. After a minute, Tanner's smile grew, and he fell into step beside the boy. When they reached a small maroon car, Tanner slid into the passenger seat. Henry was helpless to do anything but watch as Tanner left with someone else. There was no one to blame but himself. That didn't make losing Tanner any easier. Henry was always his worst enemy.

A loud knock on his window sent Henry's heart racing into his throat. The other triplet stood, waiting to be acknowledged outside. Henry patted his chest as he rolled down his window.

"Have you decided to take up stalking?"

Henry imagined it looked that way. Maybe he had. "No. It just seems I have incredibly unfortunate timing."

He rubbed the spot between his eyes where pain bloomed. "Which brother are you?"

"Toby."

"I don't suppose I can convince you to pretend you never saw me? This day has been bad enough without the extra helping of humiliation."

Toby chewed his bottom lip, visibly thinking it over. "Tell me why you're sitting here, watching Tanner leave with someone else, and I'll consider staying out of it."

That seemed fair. "I came to apologize for being a jackass earlier today. It was my bad luck I got here just in time to see him leave with someone else."

Toby held up a finger, gesturing for him to wait. As Henry looked on, Toby circled the SUV and opened the passenger side door. He hopped in with all the confidence Henry wished he possessed. "Let's go for a drive, babe. I think there are some things you need to hear about my brother."

That didn't sound ominous at all, but what choice did he have? Henry was falling for Tanner. If he ever hoped to stop fucking up, he had to start somewhere. Maybe Toby had the answer.

A mile from Howling Twister, Tanner already fought the urge to text Henry and take everything back. He couldn't do that. Being weak never worked out for him. Tanner rubbed his chest and focused on the man behind the wheel. Orion had both hands on the steering wheel like it was his sanity. His eyes were locked on the road and he couldn't have been more rigid if he tried. Tanner was a little worried Orion might pop a blood vessel in his attempt to ignore Tanner's presence.

"So, those were your work buddies. Where do you work?"

"I don't know that I would call them buddies. We had a meeting tonight and I sort of got dragged along to the bar afterward."

Tanner couldn't stop himself from teasing Orion. He was way too serious. "Well, I mean, you drove yourself. You could've just not gone, and then made up an excuse the next time you saw them."

"I drove."

A bark of laughter escaped Tanner. He tried swallowing the sound. "You just left all those people at the bar with no way home."

To his surprise, a dimple appeared in Orion's cheek. His shoulders visibly relaxed. "To be fair, I fully intend to blame you for not letting me in."

"Meh," Tanner said with a shrug. "I don't really work there, so..."

Orion cast him a quick glance before he roared with laughter. The sound shocked Tanner and made him smile. Orion was every bit as real in his laughter as he had been in his irritation. He didn't play games, Tanner surmised. Orion swiped at his eyes. "Do you have some sort of weird fetish where you start doing other people's jobs for no reason? Or was checking IDs a ploy to pick up men? If so, is this the first time it's worked?" He glanced Tanner's way again. "Never mind. I'm sure it works every time."

For a moment, Tanner questioned if he should be insulted. "None of the above," he said, deciding to let it go. "The bar is donating tonight's profits to help out a guy who was recently injured, but they needed volunteers. My brother donated his time to working the door. I was giving him a break."

"Oh. I might've stayed if I'd known about the donations. Crowds make me uncomfortable. I feel like everyone is looking at me."

"That's because you're hot."

Orion snorted. "It's because I don't fit in. I don't expect you to understand."

"Wow. You really took one look at me and decided not to like me, didn't you?"

Orion tapped his thumb on the steering wheel in his first show of nerves. "It's not that. You just seem pretty polar opposite of me. I get the impression you've never been anywhere you didn't fit in and people didn't automatically flock to you. Be honest. You've never stood on the sidelines wondering why you can't talk to anyone, have you?"

Tanner started to blow off Orion's accusations. His life had not been easy, and he felt like Orion believed it had been. But the more he thought about Orion's question, he recognized Orion was right. While Tanner's outside didn't match with his insides, he never had any problem fitting in. In fact, he was almost chameleon-like when it came to crowds.

He had learned how to survive almost anything by flirting.

"Mhmm. That's what I thought," Orion said after a moment. "You're Mr. Perfect."

Before Tanner could form a response, Orion pulled into the driveway of a small picturesque house with yellow siding, perfectly manicured lawn, and abundance of flowers. After parking, Orion led the way to the back door. Tanner kept his hands clasped behind his back and at least five feet between them. He didn't want to make Orion any more uncomfortable than he already had. After all, Orion really didn't have anything to fear and Tanner wasn't unaware of his large size. He looked just like his dad, and that man had been the master of using his size to intimidate people, especially his sons.

Orion turned lights on as he went, illuminating each room as they passed. Tanner didn't miss his chance to inspect each. The entire place was military level clean. Almost as if no one lived there. The kitchen and living room were completely void of comfort. Everything looked sterile and unwelcoming until they reached the den. Tanner knew immediately this was where Orion spent most of his time. Mismatched bookshelves lined the walls—like the man had bought a new shelf each time it was needed with zero fucks given if it looked anything like the ones he already owned. Books were stacked on the floor in front of the shelves, as if—at some point—Orion had given up trying to find places for them. There was a big recliner in the corner with an end table bursting with junk—ink pens, paper, a laptop, and empty cans lined every inch.

Since there was only one chair, Tanner moved to the closest bookshelf and eyed the titles. There didn't seem to be any particular theme or system to anything. The only similarity to any of the books was that they all seemed to be fiction. Otherwise, science fiction sat next to romance and paranormal. Shirtless men hung out next to women draped in historical dresses and the next book would have a spaceship on the cover. It seemed Orion liked everything. He spotted a familiar cover with a set of dog tags on the cover. He pulled the book off the shelf and flashed it Orion's way. "I've read this one."

Orion barely spared a glance for the book. "Yeah. That's a good one. What does the tattoo on your wrist mean?"

Tanner's gaze skirted away. "It's a weeping Willow. My mom's name was Willow."

"Was?"

Tanner nodded and focused on returning the book to its spot. "She died when I was seven."

"What happened to her?"

A humorless smile tugged at Tanner's lips. "My father killed her." Tanner dropped his hands to his sides and focused on Orion. "I mean, he never really laid a finger on her, as far as I remember, but between always being high and the constant cheating, he slowly sucked all the life from her until she faded away."

That was really what it was like to have an endless supply of money and fame. It made men feel like they could get away with anything with zero consequences and even less concern for the people they destroyed. Tanner had hated his father with something akin to insanity for a million different reasons, but for what he had to done to Tanner's mom, Tanner couldn't forgive him. Tanner shook his head. "Where's this new book?"

Orion looked almost relieved for the subject change. Tanner couldn't blame him. He never talked about his parents. Tanner didn't know why he had. Orion picked up a hardback next to his chair and passed it Tanner's way.

Tanner read the back. It didn't sound half bad. "My brother would love you," Tanner said more to himself. He glanced up. "His room looks a lot like this with books stuffed everywhere. You should come over tomorrow."

"I'm not sure that's a good idea."

Against his will, Tanner's forehead furrowed. "Why?" He thought they had gotten past this awkward stage.

Orion motioned between them. "We're very different. In my experience, different doesn't work out well for me. I'm that guy people only pursue when someone else got too hard for them." He shrugged. "I guess I look like a soft target."

Tanner fought the way Orion's words hit home. That wasn't who Tanner wanted to be, yet he was here. There was only one way he could prove Orion wrong. "Come over tomorrow."

For a solid minute, Orion chewed his bottom lip and stared at Tanner. Finally, his shoulders fell. "Give me your address. Maybe I'll come if I get bored."

A smile exploded across Tanner's lips. He would take it. Tanner needed to begin moving on somewhere. Orion seemed like a nice place to start.

Henry sat in the center of Tanner's bed and waited. If he didn't come home tonight, Henry didn't know what he would do. Go home, he supposed. There was a very real possibility that Tanner would move on and stay the night with that guy he had approached in the bar parking lot. Henry was well aware he might have screwed up for the last time. He really, really hadn't meant to hurt Tanner. Everything about them was so damn confusing, but talking to Toby helped. The guy was oddly easy to confide in, which was nuts, but whatever. Henry had obviously convinced Toby his feelings were genuine, since Toby had let him into Tanner's room to wait. Toby had been equally forthright with Henry about their childhood, shocking Henry with a few details. Now, Henry understood where he had gone wrong and he was determined to make things right. He just needed Tanner to come home and hear him out before tossing him out. That was a tall order, considering he didn't really believe he was worth keeping around. Fuck. He was in trouble.

The bedroom door swung inward and the light from the hallway hit Henry in the face. Tanner froze in the open doorway. Henry waved—like the idiot he was. "Hi. Toby said I could wait in here."

Tanner stepped inside and closed the door behind him. With his gaze averted, he tossed his keys on the dresser. "Did you pay him too?"

Henry tried not to wince at the question. "No. Actually, we took a drive and I told him all about how I'm a huge dumbass who doesn't know how to talk about my feelings. He took pity on me."

Tanner turned away and emptied his pockets on the dresser. "I've never tried to press you into talking about your feelings."

"I know, which is good because I suck at that. But I think you need me to try. I think I need to try, because I'm obviously failing you." Tanner didn't look his way. He kept his back turned, staring at the wall. Henry could practically feel the hurt rolling from him. It was now or never. "When I was your age, I fell in love with a bank manager at one of my father's banks."

Tanner ran his hands through his hair, leaving it standing on end. The way the muscles in his arms flexed distracted Henry for a moment. He finally turned. A flash of irritation crossed Tanner's face. "You broke into my room to tell me that? Thanks. Nice chat."

Henry swallowed. He wasn't used to Tanner's anger. Now, a general disappointment from everyone he ever cared about, that he was used to, but he hated Tanner's anger. "No. Sorry. I got distracted by your... never mind. Back to my story. My dad found out about my relationship with Gerard. He knew I was gay. He'd always known. I've been fabulous my whole life." Tanner didn't laugh. Henry cleared his throat uncomfortably and pressed on. "But other people knowing and seeing me with another man, that wasn't happening. That wasn't allowed. Not on his watch."

Tanner leaned back against the edge of his dresser. Even though his arms were crossed over his chest, he held Henry's stare. Henry took it as a win and kept talking.

"So, one day, he pulled Gerard aside and made Gerard an offer he couldn't refuse. If Gerard would stop seeing me, he would promote Gerard to district manager and double his salary. Or he could keep seeing me, lose his job, and Gerard would never work again. And just in case he thought to give up everything and let me take care of him, I would be disowned." Telling the story of Gerard didn't even hurt anymore. More than anything, the memory pissed him off. "Obviously, he didn't choose me. Who would have, right? But that one story, is just one of countless times that I let my father completely control every aspect of my life. I was so controlled, I may as well have been a puppet on a string. By the time he passed, five years ago, freeing me, I no longer knew how to handle relationships. The only lesson Dad ever taught me was that everyone could be bought and there was no one or nothing that couldn't be controlled for the right price." Henry took a breath. He didn't know if telling Tanner the truth helped or hurt, but Henry cared. He had to try. "Paying you. Buying that cabin to be near you. I know you don't see it, but that's the only way I know how to communicate. When we're together, you make me feel too much and confessions clog my throat, but I don't know how to say what's crushing my brain and my chest. So, I revert to what I know—money talks. If I pay you for your time, then maybe you'll see that I care about you and want to take care of you. Of course, it never works. I'm so damn frustrated with myself that when I get back to California, I spend two weeks tearing my hair out, and trying to find a way to do things right with you. It's torture, because you're perfect. You have all the words. I just have money and a shit ton of thoughts and feelings about you that I don't know how to express. Tell me what to do." Henry blinked, fighting the stinging behind his eyes. He didn't know how to save them. He didn't know how to do anything.

Tanner uncrossed his arms and crossed them again. He looked uncomfortable and angry—like a man who didn't want to hear excuses. Finally, he pushed away from the dresser. "I'd like to try something, okay? An experiment."

Henry nodded. He would do anything. "Whatever you want. Whatever it takes."

Tanner crossed the room and came to stand over him. It was a bit intimidating. "Say whatever you're thinking right now. No matter what it is. I don't care if it even has anything to do with anything we're talking about. Hell, I don't care if it's gibberish. Whatever it is, say it."

He didn't hesitate. Henry wanted to be told what to do. "I'm wondering if you kissed that boy."

Tanner's mouth lifted in one corner. "Are you having me followed?"

"No. You told me where you were going. I tried to find you so I could apologize. You were leaving with him when I got there."

"I didn't kiss him." Tanner set one knee on the bed. "What are you thinking now?"

"I'm glad you didn't."

"Why?" Tanner asked as he crawled closer.

Henry licked his lips. "Those are my kisses. I don't want to share them."

Tanner's smile grew. He straddled Henry's lap, keeping his weight balanced on his knees. Tanner kept coming until Henry was on his back with a humongous man braced above him. "Keep talking, even if the words don't make sense." Tanner kissed his jaw and neck, making it hard for Henry to focus, but he tried.

"When you left, I was so scared I wouldn't get to see you again. Actually, I'm always terrified you don't intend to see me again, because I know I'm dumb. Every time I leave without trying harder to make this real, I know I'm hurting you, but I don't know how to ask for what I want." Henry swallowed as Tanner moved lower, nibbling his collarbone.

"Keep going."

At Tanner's urging, Henry scrambled to find words. He didn't want Tanner to stop. "It's stupid, but I feel very much at your mercy. You don't need me for anything. At any time, you can walk away like you did today. You have this gorgeous house. My money means nothing. Even your family is great. All I have to offer is me and that's nothing at all."

Tanner froze with his lips pressed to the center of Henry's chest. His gorgeous green gaze lifted and fixated upon Henry's face. Even though Tanner's cheeks were flushed with desire, something darker flashed in his eyes. "You are not nothing."

The hard edge to Tanner's voice made Henry squirm. "Okay."

Tanner crawled higher. His gaze never wavered. "I don't care what you've been told in the past, or why you've come to think that, but you're mine. You don't get to think you're nothing. Understood?"

Henry nodded. His voice failed him.

Tanner didn't soften. "Don't think. Just answer honestly. What do you want?"

"You." Henry didn't have to think. That much he knew without a single doubt. He wanted Tanner, but Henry couldn't stop there. "I want you in my home and bed, where I can see you every day and know you're mine. I know that's too much too soon, but that's what I want. For once, I want to know someone I care about cares about me too."

Tanner sat back on his heels and stared down at Henry in stony silence. He didn't speak until Henry thought he would scream. "Your home is in California."

"I know."

"I can't leave my brothers, and we just started a new business."

Henry had known all of that, but it still hurt. That pain showed in his voice. "Yeah, I know, but you asked me to be honest."

Tanner's serious expression never wavered. "But I don't see why I couldn't go for a few weeks, though. Maybe if you have me under your roof, you'll finally realize that I'm in love with you and you're blind as fuck for not seeing it."

With his brain frozen, Henry didn't react. He couldn't.

Tanner's expression hardened to the point Henry couldn't read him at all. "Go ahead," Tanner taunted. "Tell me again I only want you if you buy me."

Henry swallowed—hard. "No."

Despite Henry's response, Tanner still didn't soften. "If you try to pay me again, I'm done. If you really want me, it's time to finally act like it, baby." His voice lost a bit of its hard edge, but the pain that showed in Tanner's eyes crippled Henry. "I need you to act like it," Tanner said, his voice dropping to a harsh whisper.

Henry rolled upward and wrapped his arms around Tanner's waist. With his chin tilted up, he held Tanner's stare. He needed Tanner to see he took the moment to heart. "I've never been prouder of anyone than I am you. When

I watch you talk to people, I can see your generosity and loving spirit flowing into every word and gesture. It humbles me that you would even look my way. Maybe I don't know how to express myself as good as other people, but there's no one in this entire world who wants you as much as I do. I'm sorry that I made you doubt yourself, me, and us. Please don't give up on me." Even Henry heard the desperation in his voice. He didn't care. All Henry cared about was Tanner. While he had made a ton of mistakes in his life and wasted countless years being controlled, he couldn't walk away from Tanner without knowing he had done everything in his power to hang onto him. Pride meant nothing.

"I think you should strip so we can cuddle."

Henry blinked. "We have to be nude to cuddle?"

"Well, yeah. That way, when you fall asleep in my arms, you'll be comfortable."

Henry's fingers found their way beneath Tanner's shirt. He stroked the small of Tanner's back. "Will you ever let me take care of you? I'm not talking about with money. Will it ever be my turn to make sure you've eaten or gotten enough sleep? Do I get to bring you any comfort?"

Tanner held his stare, looking as serious as always. "You're so blind."

He was, but still. "Why?"

The way Tanner's huge shoulders lifted almost distracted Henry as Tanner shrugged, but his intense stare held

Henry too captivated. "Because you can't see that you're the only warmth in my life."

There was a pressure in Henry's chest. He worried he might suffocate if Tanner didn't kiss him. "What do I need to do to convince you to kiss me?"

An evil smile tugged at Tanner's lips. "Lose at least one article of clothing. That way I know you plan to stay."

Henry fell back against the pillows and went to work on the buttons on his shirt. He wasn't going anywhere. At least, not until Tanner went with him. They were a pair. A team. Tanner needed him, and Henry wouldn't stop giving his sexy baby everything, because this was real.

Chapter Four

NO MATTER HOW HARD Tanner tried, he couldn't tear his gaze away from Henry. The way Henry stared back made Tanner think he wasn't bothered. Every word of their conversation from last night kept rolling through Tanner's mind. One thing above all the rest stood out. Henry had shown up for him. He had watched Tanner leave the bar with someone else, and he had still sat in the middle of Tanner's bed and waited. No one except his family understood how much Tanner needed that. At his core, he was a mess. He craved someone who recognized that and still loved him. Tanner had dropped all the crazy on Henry by flipping out and leaving. Henry hadn't flinched. Topping off showing up, Henry had also confided his secrets and made no attempt to have sex with Tanner. Tanner was a little thrown by that last bit.

After stripping and stealing Henry's clothes, Henry hadn't done anything beyond holding him and stealing kisses. Tanner had fallen asleep with Henry's whispered words of praise and love. There was a glow inside him now. He couldn't shake it.

"I wish you could see the way you're looking at me right now."

Tanner knew exactly how he watched Henry. He still wanted to hear Henry say it. "How am I looking at you?"

Henry's lips twitched with humor. "Like I'm one wrong move away from losing my clothes."

No matter how hard Tanner tried turning down the heat, he couldn't. "Well, I mean, this is a private plane. There's still..." he checked his watch and did the math in his head. "...a little over an hour left in this flight." He held Henry's stare. "I could do a lot in that time."

Henry stood and moved from his chair to the loveseat Tanner occupied. He had specifically chosen the seat across from Henry so he could stare at him until his heart was content. Henry straddled his hips. Tanner's arms immediately encircled Henry, pulling him closer. Sometimes, he couldn't get close enough, and now that he had finally convinced Henry his feelings were real, everything looked brighter. Tanner's heart felt ready to burst.

"You're so beautiful." The words slipped from Tanner with no input from his brain. He couldn't stop saying his every feeling.

Henry shook his head. A sweet smile touched his lips. "Tell me what would make you the happiest right now," Henry begged as he wrapped his arms around Tanner's neck.

"For you to kiss me."

Henry dipped his head and touched his lips to Tanner's. The breath caught in the back of his throat. Until their tongues met and Tanner shared Henry's air, he hadn't realized what he truly wanted. Sex was amazing and it was mind blowing with Henry, but his heart needed this. He had been so fucking starved for affection before Henry had seen his desperation and filled his life with everything he was missing. Tanner couldn't stop begging for more. He couldn't wait to get to California. Tanner needed this time with Henry to himself. He needed Henry's love, and he would find a way to win it.

The doorbell rang three times in quick succession, sending Tucker racing down the stairs. "For fuck's sake. Give me a second. Fucking doorbell never rings when everyone is home. First goddamn time I'm home alone in ages and I get the impatient stranger." He threw open the door. A skinny guy whose dark hair stuck up on end in a crazy mess—like he hadn't bothered to brush it after showering—stood on the other side. Tucker found himself eyeing his visitor from head to toe. He was tiny. Tucker wanted to pick him up just to check his weight.

The guy made a shrugging motion when Tucker didn't say anything. "You invited me here. I'm here." He didn't sound happy about it.

Tucker blinked. "No, I didn't."

The guy rolled his eyes and turned away. "I knew you were full of shit," he muttered as he walked away. "Should've gone with my gut and stayed home."

Tucker took off after him. "Hold up. Who are you here to see? There's three of us. I'm Tucker."

The irritated look the guy shot over his shoulder screamed that Tucker was full of shit. "Okay, Tucker, Tanner, or whatever your name is. Please leave me alone."

Fuck. It wasn't like Tanner to string someone along, but Tanner was definitely with someone else and on his way to California right now while this guy had obviously been invited here by him. "Seriously," Tucker called out, trying to fix what he could. "Hold up two seconds and I can prove it."

The man froze and looked up, as if seeking guidance from above before turning. "I am so stupid. Fine." He put his hands on his hips and waited.

Tucker hurriedly dug his phone from his pocket. He opened his photos on his phone and found an image of his brothers and him at the beach a few months earlier before turning the phone the guy's way. "See. I'm the one in the middle. Tanner is on the right. The other one is Toby. What's your name?"

The man's odd gray gaze slid over the picture before focusing on Tucker. He was good looking in a moody sort of way. "Orion."

It was such a fitting name. His eyes were otherworldly. Tucker smiled. "Have I at least convinced you I'm not a lying piece of shit?"

Orion's mouth lifted slightly in the corners. It wasn't a full smile. More of a smirk, but Tucker couldn't look away. "For now."

"Tanner isn't here. He got called to work." It wasn't exactly a lie. Henry was a client. Sort of. "Are you two friends?"

"No."

Orion was full of surprises. Tucker felt a bit off balance in his company. Normally, Tucker always knew what to say to bring out the flirt in everyone. This one, though, he didn't look impressed. "What brings you by, if you're not friends?"

For a moment, Orion stared at him in silence. After a second, he shrugged. "Apparently, I like wasting my time."

If Orion had any interest in Tanner, he was wasting his time. Tanner was in love with Henry. "Maybe, since you're already here, you could waste some time with me instead?"

"No, thanks," Orion said, walking away. "I think I've made a big enough fool of myself today."

Tucker had to swallow a chuckle as he went after Orion. It had been a long time since anyone told him no. He liked chasing men. Orion had made a huge misstep by catching Tucker's attention. Now, Tucker wouldn't stop until he got a taste of that fire. Tanner might be busy, but Tucker had all day.

Chapter Five

WHILE FANCY DINNERS AND charity events had gotten old a damn long time ago, Henry never tired of seeing Tanner in a tux. He was such a big guy; he should have looked uncomfortable as hell. Tanner never looked anything but amazing. Henry still preferred him nude. A smile tugged at the corners of Henry's mouth as he stared at Tanner. He had been a goner long before Tanner agreed to spend some time in California. Now, after seven of the best weeks of his life, having Tanner full-time, Henry was hopeless. He wanted to keep him. It would kill Henry when he left. That's why this was the first invitation he had accepted since Tanner came to stay. Not only did Henry not want to share a minute of Tanner with anyone, he also hated the idea of losing someone else publicly. He didn't want to explain where Tanner had gone when he walked away. Damn. Henry rubbed his chest. Tanner looked gorgeous tonight.

Tanner chewed the side of his nail, looking nervous and a bit angry. Henry followed the line of his gaze. There was a young guy, probably not more than twenty, getting felt up by an old man. It was obvious the guy had been hired to be there, and his benefactor expected more than company. The kid should be safe, considering they were sitting in a room filled with people, but Tanner was not happy. He was sweet. Henry's smile grew. A chuckle escaped him.

Tanner's gaze swung his way. "What?"

Henry motioned toward the drama. "Go. Be the hero. I know you can't take it."

A shy smile crossed Tanner's face. His ears reddened. Henry sucked in a deep breath as the pressure in his chest grew. Jesus. Tanner owned his heart. "I think I'll at least give the kid my card," Tanner said, coming to his feet. "He needs someone to have his back."

"Mhmm." It was all the response Henry could muster. He imagined they would be asked to leave soon.

Tanner leaned down and brushed his lips across Henry's. "Don't worry. I won't embarrass you."

Henry grabbed his hand before he got away. He waited until he had Tanner's attention. "You couldn't embarrass me if you tried."

With a wink, Tanner headed off to the rescue. Henry only watched long enough to enjoy the sight of Tanner's ass while he crossed the room. Then, he tried focusing on the large dining hall instead to give his eyes something to do... other than lusting over Tanner. The event was meant to raise money for suicide prevention. Turquoise and blue ribbons covered the tablecloths. That was the general theme of everything. The monotonous pattern made it hard to keep his gaze from drifting back Tanner's way. He wanted to stare at the man who owned him until his heart was content—if such a thing was possible.

"Are we still on for our meeting in the morning?"

At Gerard's sudden appearance in the chair beside him, Henry jumped. His heart slammed against the wall of his chest. "Jesus." He cleared his throat, trying to calm his nerves before focusing on the man Henry had once thought hung the moon. "Gerard. Of course. Ten tomorrow morning. I remember."

Gerard's dark blue gaze moved over Henry's face, searching for something only he knew. As always, his salt and pepper hair was perfectly styled and his tux was pristine. Henry felt nothing. "Who's your new friend?"

Henry fought the urge to look Tanner's way. "He's not new. We've been seeing each other close to a year now." Minus a few months, but whatever. Fuck, Gerard. It wasn't any of his business. "But his name is Tanner. Tanner Kodiak."

Gerard's eyebrows rose. "Any relation to Teddy Kodiak?"

"His father, actually," Henry said absently, losing his battle against looking Tanner's way. The old guy was gone, and Tanner was handing over his card. Henry couldn't help but smile at the amount of hero worship in the young man's stare. He got it. Tanner was amazing.

"Didn't he go crazy or something?"

Henry's gaze swung back Gerard's way. Irritation ran through him. "That's what they say." Honestly, Henry just wanted

Gerard to go away. "Not that it matters. He's been dead a long time."

"Huh," Gerard grunted. "Yeah, but mental illness runs in families. You might want to keep an eye out for that."

Henry went back to watching Tanner, because he couldn't stop. "I'm not worried."

As if Tanner felt Henry's stare, his head turned Henry's way. His gaze moved from Henry to Gerard and back again. Something dark passed over his features. Henry fought a hum. There was so much possessiveness in Tanner. Damn, it was hot. No one had ever shown an ounce of jealousy for him. He loved it. Tanner made him feel wanted and desirable. It was addictive. As he looked on, Tanner said something else to the guy he had rescued before heading back

Henry's way. Henry barely blinked as he watched Tanner cross the room. His hunger grew with every step. His gaze never wavered even as Tanner came to stand over him. Their fingers automatically linked as Tanner bent and touched his lips to the shell of Henry's ear.

"I can't leave you alone for a second without the vultures swooping in. You look ready to get fucked. Hard. You should let me take you home." With each word he spoke, Tanner eased Henry toward him until he had Henry on his feet. Barely an inch separated them.

"I was ready an hour ago."

Tanner's tongue traced the shell of Henry's ear. Henry's knees nearly buckled. "Home is starting to feel really far away."

Henry bit back a whimper. Tanner made him hot faster than anyone alive. "Agreed."

"The windows on that SUV of yours are pretty darkly tinted."

Goosebumps covered every inch of Henry's body. He wouldn't make it home. "They are."

A sexy chuckle rumbled against his ear. "Good. Let's find the closest empty parking lot."

Henry held tight to Tanner's arm and let him lead the way. He was fully aware he hadn't said goodbye to Gerard. Henry didn't care. He could afford to be rude. Henry couldn't afford to waste a minute of his time on anyone but Tanner.

Pleasure rippled through Tanner. His breath caught in the back of his throat. No matter how hard he tried, his heavy eyelids wouldn't lift. Sleep held him tightly in its grasp. The hot, wet tugging on his cock had Tanner writhing. His hips rolled, seeking more. He gasped for air as the suction strengthened. Soft light finally sneaked in as he fought against the deep sleep that holding Henry all night brought. He tilted his chin at an angle and stared down the line of his body, watching as Henry sucked his dick. It was a beautiful sight.

Sweat coated Henry's skin. It was obvious he had already been for his morning run. As always, Tanner had slept through Henry slipping away from the bed they shared to get his workout in before Tanner had time to miss him. Tanner hadn't realized life could be so wonderful until Henry showed him. Every day he woke to some version of heaven. Henry was amazing. Damn, he put his heart into blowing Tanner—like he loved it. Tanner buried his hands beneath his pillow, found the edge of the headboard, and held on. That was all he could do while Henry's mouth owned him. Sparks of pleasure danced on his cock, drawing his balls up tight. Tanner dug his heels into the bed and openly fucked Henry's throat. Sounds he couldn't control left Tanner's lips. Nothing mattered but reaching the orgasm Henry promised with every hollow of his cheeks. Pressure built, pounding at his crown. Tanner held his breath.

His body tensed. Henry sucked—hard. Tanner's vision narrowed. The room went silent. An explosion of pleasure and light rocked Tanner to his core. His body shook as Henry kept up the pace, drawing every last twitch of ecstasy from Tanner. While Tanner stared at the ceiling, gasping, Henry kissed his hipbone.

"Good morning, sexy."

"Damn." That one word was all that Tanner's blown mind could muster.

Henry tugged the comforter up and hid Tanner's nudity. "I need a shower. Gray will be in here any second with your breakfast."

Tanner sucked air, incapable of moving. "Fuck."

A sexy sounding chuckle followed Henry to the bathroom. Tanner knew he should chase Henry down and ensure his man was every bit as satisfied. His body refused to obey. Even as Gray silently made his way inside and quietly arranged Tanner's breakfast on the table beside the French doors, the way he always did, Tanner could only stare at the ceiling. Like everyone who worked for Henry, Gray never intruded, yet seemed to always know when it was safe to do his job. At first, it had been odd as hell having people moving about the house who pretended they weren't there. Tanner had gotten used to it after a few weeks. Now, almost two months in, and several excuses to Toby as to why he hadn't returned, Tanner sort of had a grasp on how the massive estate ran. Efficiently and without his help. The sweet smell of cinnamon wafted over Tanner. He tilted his chin and eyed the table. Gray was gone and Tanner was free to leave the bed. Tanner sat up, somewhat surprised his body still worked after Henry's attention. Of course, he had no real clue how long he had lain there, incapable of shaking Henry's spell.

Tanner leaned over the edge of the bed and found the pajama pants he had discarded last night. He pulled them on and padded across the room to eye his breakfast. Cinnamon rolls, orange juice, and coffee sat waiting. The ocean view through the French doors made the vision complete. He sat. This place felt more like home than anywhere Tanner had ever been. He knew he would have to get back to Texas and his brothers soon. It was harder than he ever dreamed, thinking about leaving Henry.

Tanner drank half his juice, hoping to wash the bitter taste away that always rose at the thought of not falling asleep with Henry every night.

The bathroom door opened, and Henry strolled out, a towel wrapped around his waist and water still rolling down his sleek body. He flashed Tanner a smile. "You're up."

Before Tanner could respond, Gray reappeared. "Excuse me, Mr. Krill. Gerard is waiting downstairs."

A deep line appeared between Tanner's eyes. "Our appointment isn't for at least another hour."

Gray's light blue eyes stayed emotionless, as always. If the man had any opinion whatsoever, he was damn good at hiding it. "Would you like me to tell him to come back in an hour?"

Henry shook his head. "No. It's fine. I'll be down there in a few."

Gray disappeared and Henry's gaze moved Tanner's way. Tanner popped a piece of a cinnamon roll in his mouth and spoke around it. "Gerard? The same one from last night?"

Henry nodded, looking annoyed.

"Is this the same Gerard you used to date?'

Henry nodded again. "My father kept him on and kept promoting him. He runs my company. We were supposed to have our quarterly meeting today. He's always early, but I really wanted to sit with you while you ate this morning."

Not to mention, Tanner still hadn't returned the favor this morning. He polished off the rest of his juice. "Come here."

Henry immediately crossed the room. The moment he was within striking distance, Tanner stole his towel. Laughter filled the air as Tanner swept Henry off his feet before planting him solidly in the center of his plate.

"Oh my god. Am I sitting on a plate of cinnamon rolls?"

"Mhmm," Tanner hummed, fighting back a laugh at Henry's horrified expression. "Now, this is the breakfast I really wanted." He pushed, tumbling Henry onto his back before going down on him. He held nothing back. When Henry left here to go spend the morning with his ex, Tanner wanted him thinking of nothing else, except the way Tanner had eaten breakfast off his ass. Tanner doubted Henry could say that about anyone else, especially the pompous twat currently waiting downstairs. Tanner was the one who loved Henry. Gerard would just have to wait.

Henry fought hard against the huge smile that owned his face. The last thing he wanted was for Gerard to think it was meant for him. It was all Tanner. Tanner owned everything, including every single thought that creeped through Henry's mind. Sometimes, Henry wanted to walk away from everything and give his undivided attention to Tanner. His family's company had been running just fine before him and would continue to do so long after he was gone. These meetings with Gerard were no more than a formality. Henry played no real role in anything and never had.

Gerard stood as Henry came through the door. "Good morning, Henry. I was beginning to think I should reschedule. I've been waiting for over an hour."

The smile tried winning again. Henry beat it back. "This is our scheduled time, is it not?" Henry asked as he moved to sit behind his desk. "Schedules exist for a reason. I had other business this morning. If you don't like waiting, then get here on time." Gerard blinked. It was beyond obvious he didn't like Henry's answer, but he was in no position to argue. Henry tried softening his tone. He was in too good of a mood for bullshit today. "Let's get started, so you're not trapped here any longer than necessary. I understand you're a busy man."

Gerard smiled. "I'm never too busy for you. You know that." Before Henry could respond, blowing off his claim, Gerard fell into a boring litany of numbers and projections.

A movement at the edge of Henry's vision caught his eye. Henry turned his head. Tanner was outside at the pool. A mini pair of swim trunks barely covered his perfect round ass. Henry subtly changed positions to get a better view. As he looked on, Tanner bent over and spread a towel over a lounge chair and set something on the ground beside it. Henry's heart rate kicked up. Tanner was so fucking beautiful. Henry never got tired of staring at him. His huge shoulders caught the sunlight as he stood. Henry's gaze followed his every move. He loved the way Tanner's muscles bunched and rolled. Lord, he was amazing. Tanner stretched out on his stomach and played with his phone. Henry's mouth watered. He wanted nothing more than to go to him right now and straddle that firm ass.

His phone buzzed, pulling his gaze away. Henry fought a smile as he saw a text appear from Tanner.

Tanner: *It's hot.*

Henry: *I see that. You probably raised the temperature by thirty degrees just by stepping outside.*

Tanner: *I could make things hotter. All I need is you to pull it off.*

"Is hearing about your money boring you?"

At Gerard's question, Henry tore his gaze away from the phone. He fought a blush. "I'm listening. If you want to sell those shares, I'm fine with that. I never felt that company would be profitable anyhow."

Obviously mollified, Gerard went back to droning on while Henry went back to staring out the window. Tanner was in the water now. Henry tapped his foot. Damn, he wanted this meeting done. Tanner swam to the edge of the pool and snagged his phone. After a moment, Henry's phone buzzed again.

Tanner: *Tell what's his name to fuck off and come kiss me.*

Henry bit the inside of his cheek. It was getting harder and harder not to smile like an idiot. His leg bounced beneath the desk. He fought the urge to run from the meeting, screaming and tearing out his hair.

His maid, Abagail, appeared in the doorway. "Excuse me, Mr. Krill. I was asked to bring this to you."

As she handed him a single red rose, Henry fought temptation. "Thank you, Abagail."

Her knowing smile had his gaze sliding away. He couldn't look at anyone. Gerard had barely paused his reading at the interruption. Henry set the rose on his desk and tried not to stare or grin like the old fool he was. His phone buzzed again. Henry's gaze automatically slid to the window. As he looked on, Tanner pushed from the pool. His muscles flexed in the most delicious way. Water streamed down his body. His already tight shorts clung to every line, showing off his bulge. Henry snapped.

He flew to his feet. "I'm sorry. I'm certain everything else is in order. If not, please see Gray to reschedule before you leave. I have something I need to take care of that can't wait."

Gerard jumped to his feet, as well. "Is there a problem? If you need me, I can stay."

Henry moved for the door without looking back. "No. It's fine. Thank you." He practically ran down the hallway the second he was out of sight. Henry burst through the patio door leading to the pool. He didn't stop moving until he stood, hovering over Tanner's lounge chair. Dark sunglasses robbed Henry from seeing if any triumph flashed in

Tanner's eyes, but his smile... goddamn. That was the devil's smile.

"Did you just walk out on your meeting?"

"You asked it of me."

A sexy sounding chuckle rumbled from Tanner. "I didn't think you'd really do it."

Confusion made Henry slow to respond. It hit him. Tanner still didn't fully get it. He didn't understand how much power he held over Henry. Henry hiked up his dress pants, threw one leg over Tanner, and settled in, uncaring of the water soaking him. The way Tanner laughed and squeezed his ass made the move worthwhile.

Henry wrapped his arms around Tanner's neck and toyed with the wet ends of his hair. "I thought you understood I would do anything for you."

"Would you?"

Henry nodded. He loved this man.

Tanner's mouth lifted in one corner, and Henry knew whatever Tanner said next would be a test. "You should marry me, then."

"Sorry to interrupt. Gray said I would find you out here."

Even as Gerard's voice penetrated Henry's cloud of shock, he couldn't look away from Tanner. "Are you being serious?"

Tanner equally ignored Gerard. "Of course. Why would I joke about something like this?"

Henry shook his head. "It's not that I think you're joking. I'm just not used to anything good happening to me."

"Even though I don't have anything pressing to discuss, I'd still like to reschedule with you, if you have the time."

A growl rose in Henry's throat. "Not now, Gerard. Reschedule with Gray."

"Oh, okay."

Henry ignored the defeat in Gerard's voice and didn't watch him go. He had more important things happening at the moment. "You would have to move away from your brothers. I thought you didn't want that."

Tanner shrugged. "I can visit and so can they. As far as the business goes, it's not like I'll be accepting anymore dates. I can network here and look out for the guys if they are working here in California—like that guy I approached last night." Tanner visibly swallowed. "You're the most important piece of me."

Henry realized he meant it. Tanner's offer was one hundred percent serious. "I love you."

Tanner didn't smile. His serious boy was back. "This is me acknowledging that's your first time saying that and I appreciate it, but I also love you enough for both of us, so it wasn't necessary."

Despite his best efforts, a laugh burst from Henry. "You're wholly unique, you know?"

Tanner shrugged. "Actually, I've just had a lot of counseling."

"No. That's not what makes your heart so beautiful. It's just you. Nothing would make me happier than marrying you." Tanner didn't smile or cheer. In fact, he sat there as if waiting for more. "As soon as possible," Henry added.

Tanner smiled. "I was waiting on a *but*. You sounded unsure."

A loud sigh escaped Henry.

Tanner used his hold on Henry's ass to haul him even closer. "I'm joking." He pressed a hard and quick kiss to Henry's lips. "I love you, sexy. You won't regret me."

"I'm not sure regretting you is even possible, no matter what. Your swim-suit is soaking through my pants. If that doesn't scream love. Nothing does."

Tanner's smile grew. He tightened his hold on Henry and stood. "Well, I mean, since you're already wet."

Horror raced through Henry as Tanner stood without letting go. "No."

An evil sounding chuckle escaped Tanner. "Oh, yeah. I think you need to be a little wetter to prove your love."

Before Henry could argue again, Tanner ran toward the pool. Henry tightened his hold on Tanner's neck and wrapped his legs harder around the man's waist as Tanner leapt through the air. He squeezed his eyes shut a split second before the water engulfed him. He nearly drowned as he came up laughing. Henry's entire body shook with happiness. Being with Tanner was like having back his youth. Henry knew in his heart, even if he lived to be a hundred, he would never feel like he had gotten enough time with Tanner. In that moment, he hated his age as much as he loved Tanner, because no amount of time would ever quench this hunger for Tanner. As their lips met and their kiss turned heated, Henry swore he would give Tanner a hundred years' worth of love no matter how much time they got together. This was his other half.

Chapter Six

TANNER: *I ASKED HENRY to marry me.*

Tucker: *And?*

Toby: *When is the wedding?*

Tucker: *He didn't say if Henry said yes.*

Toby: *Congrats! Of course, he said yes. Henry loves you.*

Tanner: *Yes, he said yes. I'll let you know about the wedding. Sorry to tell you over text, but I didn't want y'all to argue about who I called first.*

Tucker: *Good, because it would've been me.*

Toby: *Like hell.*

Tanner: ***sigh***

For several minutes, Tanner stood to the side of Henry's office door and watched him work. Honestly, Tanner didn't think he was working, per se, but he was definitely focused on something on his computer with a crazy amount of intensity. He never dreamed he could be so obsessed with anyone. In truth, when his brothers and he had decided to start Cubs for Rent, Tanner hadn't thought it would be an issue going on dates with as many people as possible with no feelings involved, because he had never fallen for a single person his whole life. Of course, there were many years he never saw anyone but his father and brothers, so he wasn't normal. Still, never in his wildest dreams had Tanner expected to feel so much love for one person. Henry glanced up, catching him staring. He blushed.

Tanner smiled so hard at the sight that his cheeks ached from it. "Why are you blushing? Did I catch you watching porn?"

With a chuckle, Henry shook his head and motioned for Tanner to join him. "I've been looking at rings, but I can't find anything. It's not like me to be this picky." He shook his head again. "I don't know. There's just something missing in every one of them."

Tanner dragged a chair next to Henry and glanced at the screen. He kept his eyes locked on the computer, even as he passed a single red rose Henry's way. Tanner didn't look to see how it was received. The only thing he cared about was making Henry happy. After a moment, he leaned back and dug through his pocket, finding the reason he had been hovering in the first place. He set the ring box on the desk in front of Henry. "Maybe it's because those rings aren't the ones I bought for you."

For a moment, Henry stared at the box in silence before meeting Tanner's gaze. "You bought rings?"

Tanner nodded. "I'd been planning to ask you the right way for a while now.

Honestly, I don't know what happened yesterday. It just sort of popped out. Sorry you didn't get a better proposal."

"It was perfect," Henry said, giving him a quick kiss. He reached for the box and Tanner held his breath. The rings were actually a bit simplistic, but he thought they were perfect. Henry popped open the box and stared at the contents in silence.

Tanner broke. "If you don't like them, I can exchange them for something different."

Henry ran the tip of his finger across the two bands. One was a thin gold band with a tiny diamond sunk into the ring. The other was a wider band to match. Henry still didn't speak.

Tanner's nerves frayed. "The thinner one is meant to be worn now as an engagement ring. The other is your wedding band to add to the other on our wedding day. They kind of lock together. Still, if you don't like them..." His leg bounced. Tanner tried to sit still.

"They're perfect." Henry met Tanner's stare. "I'm just really moved." His voice sounded strained—like Tanner really had wowed him. "I've been looking at rings all morning, kind of frustrated because nothing felt right but I didn't know why. You're right. It's because they weren't from you. Now I just have to find you a set," he added with a laugh.

The sound made Tanner's stomach muscles clench with desire. "I'm getting you in this marriage. Anything else is just icing, so don't stress." Tanner swiped his hands on his thighs. "Try it on."

The way Henry smiled—like a kid with a new toy had Tanner matching his happiness level. Henry slipped the set on. It fit perfectly. Tanner couldn't help but feel like it was yet another sign they were meant to be. "Leave them on," Tanner said before he could stop himself. He couldn't watch Henry take off the rings. "Let's go to Vegas." He couldn't stop. Desperation owned him. "I want the world to know you're mine." Plus, he was scared shitless Henry would change his mind.

"I'll concede to half your request. I won't take off the rings, but I want a real wedding. Don't worry," he said before Tanner could argue. "I'm not talking about a year of planning or anything crazy like that. Like you, I want to be married as fast as possible, but I also want all the fanfare. I want the engagement party where I get to show off how lucky I am, and the gorgeous wedding that has everyone talking. You're the best thing that's ever happened to me. I want everyone to know it."

As much as Tanner wanted to argue, Henry looked happy. He couldn't deny him this. "Whatever makes you happy, I'm in. Just promise me you won't stress yourself out, okay? This is supposed to be happy and I want you to enjoy it. Don't try so hard to make it perfect that you don't get to experience it."

"Promise. Give me two weeks to pull this off and I swear we'll be married. No stress."

Tanner took a breath. He didn't want to wait, but he would for Henry. "I'm not going anywhere."

Henry pulled a worried face. "What do you think your brothers will say? I'm a lot older than you."

"They're thrilled," Tanner rushed to assure him. "I told them this morning. We know one another better than anyone. They know I wouldn't have asked you if this wasn't real. Toby and Tucker will stand behind us no matter what."

A sad smile tugged at Henry's lips. "It must be nice to have people in your corner."

"It's our corner now." Tanner needed Henry to know they were a team. He was Henry's family now.

Henry made an impatient gesture, as if recalling something important. "Speaking of your brothers, I've been thinking, I'm not really needed here much. How do you feel about splitting our time? We

147

have the cabin in Texas. Let's live there part of the year."

Hope nearly crushed Tanner's chest. "But California is your home."

"So? Texas is yours. If you can uproot your life for me, I can do it for you. I want you to be close to your brothers. Plus, the cabin is smaller and cozy. We're right on top of each other, and that's always fun."

Tanner shook his head. He was blown away by Henry. "I have no idea how I got so lucky, but I really fucking love you. You're amazing." For a long moment, they simply stared at each other, as if equally blown away by the knowledge they had found each other. Out of nowhere, an overwhelming sense of regret washed over Tanner. Henry deserved so much better than he was getting. Tanner was half crazy and had a past he couldn't tell anyone. Henry deserved to know that before he tied his life to Tanner. "I'm sorry about how I acted last time we were at the cabin. I mean, I don't regret we got things straightened out, but I'm sorry you fell in love with someone who's not particularly good at life." He wasn't expressing himself well and that was pretty par for course with Tanner. It frustrated him. "No doubt there were a million different ways I could've handled my anger better, but I was never allowed to be upset growing up." Tanner struggled to explain without saying too much. "My brothers and I had to be as invisible as possible, because it was safer when we didn't draw attention to ourselves." Tanner fought a growl. He didn't know how to say what he wanted to say. "I probably could have done better."

Henry grabbed his hands and held on, steadying Tanner. The pressure eased in his chest at the understanding and strength in Henry's eyes. "I trust you." Tanner took a breath at Henry's claim. The air felt lighter. Henry didn't stop. "We needed to learn how to talk to each other and we did. That's all that matters. We both obviously had fathers that left their mark, but I think we're better people than they were. I don't think it's possible for you to ever disappoint me. You're pretty much the only reason I get up every day."

"I never would've accepted your father's bribe." His sudden confession dragged a laugh from Henry just as Tanner hoped, but he was serious. He snagged Henry's waist and hauled Henry into his lap. "I would rather live penniless and in a tent with you than have a dime. Trust me, I've lived in a tent. I can do it. Your dad wouldn't have stood a chance against me. I would've had him tearing his hair out, because you're mine. There's not enough money in the world to replace you." He kissed Henry's neck, blowing against his skin and making noises that had Henry laughing harder. His kisses turned sweet until his lips barely brushed Henry's skin. Tanner's heart was full.

Henry settled deeper into Tanner's hold. "I would've let him disown me for you. We could've run away where neither your father nor mine could find us and you would've kept us safe. But I have to say, thank god I didn't have to make that choice, because now I get to spend his money on the one thing that would've killed him, getting married to the man of my dreams. So, fuck the past."

Tanner couldn't stop smiling. He didn't say it, but Tanner's dad would have hated that Tanner was marrying a rich man. Both their fathers were probably spinning in their graves. But like Henry said, fuck the past. They had survived to find each other. They were a goddamn miracle.

Chapter Seven

WHILE LISTENING TO THE phone ring, Tanner chewed on the side of his nail. He had waited too long to make this call, but it needed to be done. Finally, after the fourth ring, Legend's sexy voice tumbled through the line. "Hello, there, gorgeous. It's nice to see your name appearing on my phone."

"Flirt."

Legend chuckled at the accusation.

Tanner smiled at the sound. He couldn't avoid this any longer. Legend was his friend. "So, I have news and I'm not sure how it'll be received."

"Oooh, a confession. Do tell. Does this have anything to do with you dating Henry?"

For a moment, Tanner floundered. "I didn't realize you knew that, but yeah."

Legend snorted. "Um, one of your brothers is a shameless gossip." *Tucker*. "And he knew I wouldn't care. I love you and Henry truly is a great guy. He just wasn't *my* great guy. I'm glad he found you, but I'm even happier for you. You deserve to have someone who will shower you with affection. Henry will definitely do that."

Tanner smiled into the phone like an idiot. He was ridiculously happy. "Well, you knowing about Henry makes things easier, since there's more. We're getting married."

"Whoa," Legend breathed, sounding blown away. "I never thought I would see the day any of the Kodiak boys would tie the knot. Congratulations. Make sure you let Henry know how happy I am for you both."

Tanner fought the urge to chew on his nail again. "You could tell him yourself if you're willing to come to our wedding next week."

Silence met his words. Tanner fully expected to get shot down. Finally, Legend cleared his throat. "Sure. Wow. That's... wow. Just let me know. Do I need to book a flight to Texas? I can do whatever you need."

"It's here. That's another reason I called. We plan to live here in California a majority of the year, but I need to still pull my weight with the business. I can't leave everything on Toby and Tucker's shoulders. How do you feel about introducing me to some guys out here who might be interested in working for us?"

Legend didn't hesitate. "I'm in. Whenever you want to get together, I can think of a few people."

Legend never let him down, which really, that knowledge doubled Tanner's guilt. "Are you positive I haven't made things weird? Your friendship means a lot to my brothers and me."

"Stop," Legend said, sounding firm. "Look, the thing with Henry was as much my fault as it was his. I was falling for Pytor and Yaro at the time, and that was scary as hell. Henry felt like the safe choice and he deserved better than to be my escape plan. Honestly, I think this whole thing just proves there's a bigger plan for us all. If Henry hadn't felt the need to chase me to Texas to apologize, he never would have met you. Everything happened exactly how it should so I could end up where I am, and you could end up where you're supposed to be. Tucker says it's beyond obvious that Henry is head over heels for you, which is high praise coming from him. That's a beautiful thing. I can't wait to see you both."

Tanner dragged a deep breath into his lungs. He had been putting off talking to Legend for so long that it seemed odd to have everything off his chest, but he felt better. "I can't wait to see you too, and those sexy men of yours. I'll text you with the wedding details, okay?"

"Sounds good. Now that I know you're in town, don't be a stranger, okay?"

"I won't. Talk to you soon."

"See ya," Legend said, disconnecting their call.

Tanner shook his head. He was a bit amazed that things had gone so well. In truth, he had also been a little worried that talking to Legend would stir some jealousy inside him. It was ridiculous. Legend didn't want Henry, but Henry had asked Legend to marry him. Tanner didn't want that knowledge to come between them. Unfortunately, Tanner wasn't always reasonable.

"Excuse me, Mr. Tanner."

Tanner set his cellphone aside and turned at Gray's sudden appearance. He couldn't fight the chuckle rising in his throat over being called Mr. Tanner. "How many times do I have to tell you, it's okay to just call me Tanner."

Gray nodded the way he always did every time they had this conversation. "I don't like to overstep more than once in the same conversation, and I plan to overstep."

"Of course. Where's the fun in holding back?" Before Gray was forced to search for a polite way to sidestep Tanner's question, Tanner moved on. "What can I help you with, Mr. Gray?" Tanner didn't know why he always had to fuck with Gray. The man was a professional at his job, for sure. Maybe that's what made it so much fun.

Gray's chest expanded, fascinating Tanner. Tanner had never seen Gray look uncomfortable. He was seeing it now. "I'm sorry for speaking out of turn, Mr. Tanner, but the staff and I really like you. You make Mr. Krill smile and laugh. None of us ever saw that before you got here."

"Thank you. I like everyone here too."

Gray gave him a sharp nod, acknowledging his words. "That's why we are excited about your upcoming wedding and feel you should know that the slimy Gerard is downstairs alone with Mr. Krill."

Gray's warning solidified Tanner's growing unease about Henry's ex. "Huh. I thought maybe it was just jealousy that had me hating that guy's face."

Henry's personal assistant shook his head. "It's not just you. He's not a good person. As Mr. Krill's employee, I'm not at liberty to say as much to Mr. Krill, but Gerard is no good and I'm always worried when he's alone with Mr. Krill."

Just the fact that Gray only used Gerard's first name proved how little respect the staff had for the man. Tanner wanted to know everything. "Tell me everything."

Gray's chest expanded again on another deep breath and Tanner knew he wouldn't like what he was about to hear. But Tanner knew he needed to hear it. He just hoped it was a quick story, because he had the love of his life to save.

By force of will and distraction, Henry managed to make it through his rescheduled meeting with Gerard. While he had only listened with half an ear, since he had been trying to choose a wedding gift for Tanner that wouldn't send him running for the hills, Henry still didn't understand why Gerard had insisted upon rescheduling at all. It was all boring bullshit that didn't require his attention.

The moment Gerard declared himself finished with his report, Henry pounced. "I can never tell if I'm being over the top. Keeping that in mind, which of these things sounds less outrageous to you—a month long stay at a private resort in Fiji or a car?"

Gerard blinked at Henry like he had lost his mind. Henry propped up his chin with his fist and waited. This was a wedding gift. It had to be perfect.

"Fiji," Gerard said after a minute. "It's harder to guess the price tag on that one. Who are you..." Gerard's eyes widened as he trailed off. "Are you wearing a wedding band?"

Henry didn't know why he looked at his hand at the question. He just kind of liked the sight of his rings. Henry felt like he owned the world each time he caught sight of them. "Oh, actually it's an engagement ring. Well, it's my wedding band too, but I guess I forgot to tell you, I'm getting married. The wedding is next week. You're invited. In fact, I have your invitation to the engagement party and wedding in here somewhere," he said absently while shifting through the piles of invitations and everything else covering his desk. He found Gerard's. "Ah ha. Here you go."

Even though Gerard reached for it, he looked like he expected to get bit. "You're getting married next week? To Tanner? Are you being serious?"

Henry's eyebrows snapped together. "Why would I joke about something like that?"

Gerard didn't open the invitation. Instead, he stared at Henry with open challenge. "Do you even know this guy?"

A snort escaped Henry without thought. "He lives here. We spend every waking moment together. That's knowing someone."

"Henry," Gerard said, sounding condescending. "You can live with someone for years and not know them. You should probably—at the very least—have him investigated and start working on a prenup. You can't do that in a week."

A burble of laughter rose in Henry's throat. "Don't be ridiculous."

Gerard stared at Henry like he questioned Henry's sanity. Maybe he had gone crazy, but fuck it. Henry had never really cared about the money. He knew Tanner didn't want his money, but so what if he did? Tanner could have it.

"Which part am I being ridiculous about?" Gerard asked, sounding offended. "You have to protect your company. People depend on you for their jobs."

Henry bit back a sigh. "Everything you've said so far today is completely ludicrous. First off, even if Tanner divorces me and takes half of everything, I'll still be one of the richest men alive. So, don't worry. Your job is safe. As far as an investigation goes, that's dumb. Tanner and I talk about everything. If I want to know something, I'll ask. He's not a liar. I'm not undermining our relationship by acting like my dad."

"Are you joking? Do you even hear yourself?" Gerard looked apoplectic. "He could be a con man. For all you know, he's already married three millionaires and killed them. You know nothing about this man."

Henry rolled his eyes. "Are you finished? I'm trying to figure out the perfect wedding gift."

"See? How much are you spending on this wedding? He already has you pissing away your money."

"It was my idea," Henry said, getting irritated. "He wanted to get married in Vegas. I'm the one who insisted on all this grand scale crap, which—honestly—I'm starting to regret. I should've run off with him when he suggested it. This is a lot more stressful than I expected, and I'm seriously over it."

"He tried to get you to run away to Vegas? And that didn't set off any warning bells? Someone who loves you for you would be willing to wait."

Henry shook his head. "He *is* willing to wait, which led to my regret in asking him to do so. Keep up and pick a thing to be angry about. You're starting to sound like you're just trying to stop me from being happy. Do you know who you sound like? You sound like my dad."

Gerard drew back, looking hurt. "Is that what you think?"

Henry didn't back down. "I don't know. Is that what I should think?"

"No," Gerard said, sounding sincere. "I've always only wanted your happiness. You know I care about you. A lot," he added, sounding like Henry had truly hurt his feelings.

Henry called his temper back under control. He didn't want to fight. "You're a good friend. I know your heart is in the right place, but please don't interfere in this. Tanner is pretty spectacular, and he really does love me. With my dad being the man he was, I never thought I'd have this. I do now and I'm giving it my everything. So, stay out of it. Tanner is worth it."

Gerard nodded but didn't have a chance to say anything more. Tanner sailed through the door, looking like the sexiest man on the planet to Henry. "Hey, hottie. Gray said you were finished in here." He stepped around Gerard and snagged Henry from his chair. Before Henry could react, he found himself over Tanner's massive shoulder. A burst of laughter escaped Henry as Tanner stepped around Gerard again. "Excuse me. Nice to see you again. Sorry, I forget your name. I'm just retrieving my property. Gray says he'll see you out."

Henry covered his mouth, trying to stifle his laughter as Tanner strolled from the room, carrying him away. He really loved this ridiculous guy who had taken over his world. Tanner always knew exactly how and when to save him.

At the stairs, Tanner shifted Henry in his arms until he cradled the man against his chest before heading up toward their room. He fought the urge to stare at the love of his life. The last thing Tanner wanted was to trip and kill them. At the moment, he was too hungry and possessive. Henry belonged to him. He wouldn't let anyone come between them.

"Caveman."

A smile exploded across Tanner's face. All his anger melted away at Henry's accusation. "Maybe." He met Henry's gaze as he crossed the threshold of their bedroom. As he held Henry's stare, Tanner kicked the bedroom door closed behind him. "But you're mine and I want you. I got tired of waiting."

A flush rose on Henry's cheeks. His gaze dropped to Tanner's mouth. "I want you too."

That was all the permission Tanner needed. He headed for the bed and gently set Henry on the mattress. While holding Henry's gaze, Tanner stripped. He loved watching the lust grow in Henry's eyes. Once he was nude, Tanner went to work on Henry's clothes. He didn't let Henry do anything. Tanner was in seduction mode. He didn't want Henry to have any regrets about keeping him. Tanner needed Henry way more than Henry would ever need him. It was important to Tanner for Henry to feel his worth.

"You're so unbelievably sexy. Inside and out. I'm so proud to be marrying you."

Tanner felt Henry's praise all the way to his soul. He kissed Henry's stomach. "You have no idea how humbled I am by you. I don't deserve you, but I won't ever stop trying." His lips moved to Henry's hipbone. Henry's fingers brushed through his hair. Tanner licked Henry's crown before moving away. He dug the lube from the bedside table before crawling onto the bed. Tanner had every intention of fucking Henry's sexy ass, but he wanted that dick in his mouth first. He wanted to keep Henry so high he didn't have time to think about Gerard.

Tanner snagged Henry's legs, dragged him closer, and swallowed his cock. Henry's hips left the bed, chasing the euphoria Tanner promised. Tanner took no mercy. He hollowed his cheeks and sucked, taking all of Henry with each draw. Henry babbled and begged. Tanner didn't let up. When he felt Henry stiffen and Henry yanked his hair, Tanner only worked harder. A cry bounced from the walls as Henry's cum filled Tanner's mouth. Satisfaction roared through Tanner as he crawled up Henry's body and claimed Henry's mouth. To his surprise, Henry pushed at his chest until he had Tanner on his back. He coated Tanner's cock with lube, making Tanner pant with desperation. Tanner was turned on to the point of being painful. He wanted to tear at his skin. Before Henry, Tanner hadn't known what it was like to want one person so badly. With his erection shimmering with oil, Henry straddled him and impaled himself on Tanner's dick.

"Jesus," Tanner breathed, trying not to come right then.

Henry bit his shoulder. His short nails tore at Tanner's skin as he rode Tanner's cock like it was the only drug that got him high. All Tanner could do was suck air and take it while praying he didn't disappoint the man who owned his heart. Tanner's entire body seized. His brain glitched. Henry's name tore from his lips as his body shook from the power of the orgasm Henry pulled from him. Tanner swore he lost part of his soul.

"Fucking perfect," Tanner growled as he claimed Henry's mouth. He had never meant anything more in his life. This man was his and there was no low he wouldn't stoop to in order to keep Gerard away. Next time, Tanner was likely to fuck Henry on the desk in front of him just to prove a point. It was time for Gerard to back away.

Chapter Eight

ONCE TANNER STOOD IN the middle of the gorgeous engagement party Henry put together, he had to admit it was nice. He was moved. Not only had a ton of people shown up to support them, Tanner recognized Henry had done this for them. Henry was proud of what they had together. Everything Henry did solidified Tanner's belief in him a little more every day. Henry was the love he had been denied since his mother's death. Tanner couldn't imagine a life without him.

Henry squeezed his hand. "You're being very quiet tonight. I know you hate crowds, but—"

Tanner kissed him, cutting off whatever Henry had been about to say. Several people nearby clapped and someone wolf whistled. Henry smiled against his lips. Tanner held Henry's face between his hands, so he couldn't look away. "I'm quiet because I'm blown away. You put a lot of work into making this perfect."

Henry shrugged. "I love you. I know most people would've hired someone else to do this, but I love you," he repeated as if that summed up everything. Tanner supposed it did.

"That's why I'm speechless," Tanner said, stealing another kiss because he had to. "You're perfect. Can I get you some more champagne?" Henry looked ready to drop. Between planning everything on super short notice and spending the entire night on his feet, talking to every guest, Henry needed to be babied. Tanner wanted the job.

Henry fanned his face. It was getting pretty hot with so many people crowded inside their home. "Please. Honestly, I'm sort of hoping people start leaving soon. I'm frying and exhausted."

Tanner nodded. He briefly considered tossing everyone out before deciding he couldn't ruin Henry's party. "Give me a minute to grab you a drink. If people don't start trickling out soon, I'll give them a show."

Henry's laughter made Tanner smile as he walked away. He was completely serious. Tanner wasn't above making an ass of himself.

"I love seeing that smile, baby brother."

Tanner released a loud sigh he didn't really feel. "You never intend to let that nineteen minutes go, do you?"

Toby shrugged. "Something has to set the three of us apart. My being the oldest is my only claim to fame. You get to be the baby. Tucker, well... he gets to be the loudest."

"Where is Tucker, anyhow?" Tanner asked, casting a quick glance around. "I only got to talk to him for a few minutes earlier before he disappeared.

"Last time I saw him, he was on the phone. I think he stepped outside. It's getting pretty toasty in here with Henry and you kissing every two minutes."

Tanner rolled his eyes, but he was too happy to care.

Toby slapped him across the back. "You know I'm just fucking with you. It's good to see you happy. I never thought I would."

"Thanks," Tanner grumbled as he motioned for a glass of champagne from the bartender.

"It's nothing personal," Toby said moving closer. "I never expected any of us had the mental equipment it takes to produce happiness." The bartender handed Toby a glass too and he nodded his thanks. "I thought the ability to be happy had been beaten out of us years ago. It's good to be proven wrong. Maybe there's still hope for Tucker and me." Damn. Tanner wanted that. He craved seeing his brothers whole and smiling when it wasn't faked. Toby drained his glass in one swig and set it aside. "Anyhow, I think I'll go find Tucker and get some fresh air. It's too crowded in here for my tastes." With another slap across Tanner's back, Toby disappeared into the crowd.

Tanner grabbed Henry's champagne and started back toward Henry only to find his path blocked by Gerard.

"I hoped to catch you alone for a moment."

"Okay." That was all Tanner had. If Gerard possessed an ounce of sense, he wouldn't want to catch Tanner alone at all. They might not find Gerard's body.

"We need to talk about Henry."

Tanner's eyebrows rose. "What about him?"

181

Gerard surprised him by not immediately backing down. Tanner was easily twice his size and half his age. Gerard either didn't notice or thought his money would save him—like most rich pricks did. "I've been waiting a long time to be with Henry. Don't think I plan to let this wedding go through. He deserves better than some kid who spends all day distracting him from the fact that you're after his money."

A chuckle burst from Tanner. It sounded as evil as Tanner felt. This guy didn't know him. Tanner would fucking see Gerard dead before he let the man hurt his relationship. "Have you been waiting?" Tanner asked, sounding condescending even to his ears. "Because, I have got to say, Henry's father has been dead for like five years now. Where have you been all that time?" Before Gerard could respond, Tanner cut him off with a snap of his fingers. "Oh, yeah. You were married for twenty years to some poor woman who had no clue you preferred men until you divorced her the minute Henry's father was in the ground. Unfortunately, for you, she didn't go quietly so you were stuck waiting through a long, ugly divorce." He could tell Gerard was shocked by the depth of his knowledge, but Tanner wasn't finished. No one fucked with Tanner's life. "Or," he said, being extra obnoxious. "You haven't decided yet if you should tell Henry the real reason his father came between you two. But, I have to say, I'm not sure if telling Henry you were fucking his dad is a good way to start a relationship you supposedly care so much about." Tanner kept a feral smile in place while driving in as many nails as possible in Gerard's coffin. He wasn't playing around. "You see, the thing is, Gerard, you're weak. You were weak all those years ago when Henry's father promoted you for sucking his dick, and you haven't stopped being a pussy since. So, forgive me if I'm not running for the hills at your threat. I just don't see you as one." Another evil chuckle rumbled from Tanner as he walked away. Tanner truly didn't see the man as a threat, but the guy had openly challenged him. That was more than Tanner had expected from such a self-serving bastard. Usually, snakes stayed hidden. Tanner had to step up his game. That was fine. He had this.

Tanner handed Henry his champagne.

Henry's eyes flashed with happiness. "Thank you. What were you talking about with Gerard? I've only seen you look that silently enraged a couple of times. It never stops being sexy."

Tanner shrugged. "He was saying he'd been waiting a long time to be with you and wouldn't let this wedding go forward. I was threatening his life."

Henry froze with his champagne halfway to his lips. "Are you being serious?"

Oh, he was. Gerard thought he was dealing with a child who didn't feel secure enough to talk to Henry. Little did Gerard know; they had already suffered all the setbacks Tanner would tolerate. Now, they talked about everything. "Unfortunately, I'm being very serious." Rage flashed in Henry's eyes. It was so fucking sexy. "Damn. I should've told you sooner that I suspected this was coming with him. Your anger is hot as hell."

Henry blinked. "You thought this might happen?"

Tanner shrugged. "Yeah. He looks at you just like I do—like you're everything."

The way Henry softened had Tanner fighting the urge to kiss him. They had bigger issues right now. Henry turned up his champagne, emptying the glass. "No sense in letting good alcohol go to waste." He set the glass aside. "Now, shall we?" he asked, taking hold of Tanner's bicep.

Tanner couldn't stop smiling and even he didn't know why. All he knew was, Henry would make him proud. "Where are we headed, gorgeous? This is your party."

"Exactly," Henry said with a sharp nod. "I planned this event and I can leave it. Gray will make sure everyone finds their way home or to their assigned rooms. Let's find your brothers and head to Vegas."

For a moment, Tanner could only stare at Henry and blink. When he realized Henry was serious, and they were truly headed to Vegas to get married, Tanner threw his head back and roared with laughter. He loved this man. Henry was such a warrior. Tanner swiped at his eyes. "Oh, sexy. We're going to have such a beautiful life."

"I know," Henry said while holding his stare. Tanner believed in them. They would be great.

It was funny how—when it came right down to it—Henry knew exactly who he could trust. Deep down, he had always known Gerard wasn't on that list. But as he spotted Legend across the room, speaking closely to the ear of one of his men, Henry knew Legend was one of those people he could always count on too. At first, it had been odd seeing Legend there with his husbands. Even though he felt nothing for him, and he knew Legend was a friend of Tanner's, it was still strange to see his face tonight. Now, Henry had never been happier, because Legend had married the kind of men who cared little for the law or rules, and Henry needed that right now.

With Tanner held in his grasp, Henry headed straight for Legend. Legend must have seen something in Henry's face, because he didn't hesitate. "What do you need?"

Henry would remember this favor for the rest of his life. "We need to gather Tanner's brothers and make our way to Vegas."

Legend nodded, looking serious. "Eloping. Got it. Yaro will drive. He has years of experience at getting his boss out of places he doesn't want to be. Pytor will grab the brothers, and I'll find an SUV in the garage big enough for all of us while you call your pilot." Legend's huge husbands, Pytor and Yaro nodded along, obviously completely willing to help.

Henry felt moved to give them an out. "You don't have to come along, if we're asking too much."

"We will come," Pytor said in his usual thick Russian accent. "Legend will be hurt if he cannot see you wed. I will get the cubs and meet you outside."

At Henry's nod, everyone moved in opposite directions except Tanner and Henry. They held onto each other while heading for the back door. They almost made it.

Gerard stepped into their path. His dark blue gaze locked on to Henry and didn't budge. "May I speak to you in private?"

"He is busy," Yaro said, appearing like a large guardian angel and swooping between them. No matter how Gerard fought to get around him, Yaro blocked his path. Yaro had been a bodyguard for a mafia boss for thirty years. Gerard didn't stand a chance. Henry had never been more grateful in his life. Before Tanner, Henry had been lonely and too scared to do anything about it. Tanner made him brave and filled his life with laughter. No one would steal that from him. At the moment, nothing mattered more than making Tanner his forever. But when they got home, Henry fully intended to fire Gerard. No one fucked with the other half of his soul. Henry was finished with people stealing his happiness.

Chapter Nine

No matter how hard he tried, Henry couldn't stop staring at Tanner. He had done it. Tanner had married him. Henry couldn't believe it. It was almost funny, but until Tanner had looked at him with his heart in his eyes and repeated his vows, there had been a small part of Henry that hadn't believed Tanner could possibly love him. He did. Suddenly, a month-long trip to Fiji, so they could hide out from the world, didn't seem like a good enough wedding gift.

Henry needed to give Tanner more. He needed to give him everything.

"I'd like for you to take my last name." Tanner froze. His gaze turned from heated to visibly hanging on Henry's every word. Henry couldn't stop there. "Also, I've been thinking about the whole Gerard thing, and I realize now he always made me do a lot of unnecessary work just so he could hang around. I'm not really needed in California. We should move to Austin full-time. I want you to have your brothers."

Tanner shifted positions in the gigantic bubble bath they shared. He snagged Henry's waist and towed him forward until Henry straddled his lap. "You can't leave your staff behind. They would be heartbroken. You are their family. Gray would be crushed."

He was perfect. Henry couldn't love him more. "We won't leave them. They'll come too. If we make the move permanent, we'll need a much bigger place than the cabin." His hands slid from where they were braced on Tanner's chest to the edge of the tub behind Tanner as Henry shifted even closer until their erections bumped. "What do you say, Tanner Krill? Would you like to start a whole new life with me? New name. New home. Same old man."

"*Pssh*. Old man, my ass. You haven't stopped wearing me out since we met." Heat exploded through Henry's face at Tanner's claim. Tanner chuckled and kissed the tip of his nose. "I'm not complaining. I can't get enough." He changed angles and brushed his lips across Henry's. "I'd love to stay near my brothers, but I also love making you happy. If you seriously want to move, and you're not just doing it to make me happy, then yes. But I need you to be happy too. California is your home. Wherever you are, that's my home." He swiped another kiss across Henry's lips, slowly seducing him with tiny touches. "As to your last name, I absolutely want that. Belonging to you is the best part of me."

Henry's throat swelled. Belonging to Tanner was the best part of him too. He swallowed past the emotions over-whelming him, but his feelings showed in his voice when he tried to speak. "I never expected to have you."

Tanner nodded, looking solemn. "Same. I thought my dad had beat-en any ounce of humanity that any-one could possibly love from me."

Henry held his breath. Tanner never talked about his father. Everything Henry knew, he knew because of Toby. Henry didn't press. He held still, ready to listen. Tanner visibly swallowed. "But here you are," Tanner said in a whisper, as if incapable of speaking any louder.

"You will have the best life. I promise." Henry meant the words to the bottom of his soul. He would take care of Tanner. Nothing bad would ever happen to him again. He touched his lips to Tanner's. "Love you so much."

Tanner drew Henry's hand to his, flattened his palm against Henry's, and linked his fingers with him. It was the first time they had held hands with Tanner wearing his wedding ring. The knowledge filled Henry with pride. Tanner looked completely focused on Henry. "I love you too. You should go to bed with me."

Henry faked affront. "Who is wearing out whom?" Even as he joked, Henry stood. He wouldn't miss a chance to crawl into bed with his sexy husband. Before he could fully exit the tub, Henry found himself sitting on the edge with his dick in Tanner's mouth. Henry clung to Tanner's shoulders while Tanner blew his mind. This was how things always were with them. One second, Henry would be doing the most innocuous thing. The next, he was in a sexual haze while Tanner stole his soul. Henry didn't want it to ever stop.

The moment Henry thought he might beg for release, Tanner shot to his feet. As he stepped out of the tub, he swept Henry into his arms and headed for the bed. Tanner was back in serious mode. His jaw was hard, and his eyes looked determined. Henry took a slow and steadying breath. If he knew nothing else, Henry knew he was about to get thoroughly fucked. His heart was fuller than it had ever been. Nothing mattered anymore except this man who had swept in and saved him almost a year ago. That night he hadn't realized how much he had needed to be rescued. As Tanner settled between Henry's thighs, holding his stare with all the same intensity inside Henry's heart, Henry sent up a prayer of thanks. Someone had been looking out for them that night and had seen the desperation in their souls before thrusting them together. Henry fully believed that. That was the only explanation for such a perfect match. Henry would never take this man for granted. Tanner would always know love and affection in Henry's care. Tanner would have the happy ending he deserved.

It was a bit weird being back under the same roof as his brothers. Tanner never expected that. With their new home under construction, Tanner and Henry had decided to split their time between packing up in California and enjoying Tanner's old bedroom in Texas. Tanner bit back a smile as he brought his coffee cup to his lips. They did have some delicious memories of that bed.

"What's that smile all about?" Henry asked as he carried his cup to the table.

Tanner shook his head. "Just wondering if we should have a special room in the new house for my old bed. You know, for midday trysts and nostalgia."

Henry's mouth lifted in one corner and Tanner knew he was thinking about their first night together too. Tanner would always believe for the rest of his life that they had been a case of instant love. They had been meant to meet. Fated long before they knew each other existed. Every memory they made was beautiful.

The doorbell rang, dragging Tanner's gaze away from eating Henry alive. "Damn. I'm probably closest. Wow. I miss Gray."

"Just a few days more," Henry promised. "He'll be with us again."

Tanner winked as he pushed to his feet. He carried his cup with him to the front door, sipping as he went. The doorbell rang twice more in quick succession. "Yeah, yeah. Patience is a virtue," Tanner grumbled as he pulled the door open. For a moment, he blinked at the guy standing on the other side.

Orion rubbed his arm, looking uncomfortable as hell. His gaze shot from side to side, avoiding Tanner. "You know I don't like it when you stare at me."

"Um, no, I didn't know that."

Orion's crazy colored stare finally landed on him and didn't budge. "Oh. You're not Tucker."

"You're here for Tucker?" Even Tanner heard the disbelief in his voice. It was just that the whole situation was odd as hell. He had completely forgotten about

Orion, and now here he was...looking for Tucker.

A stampede of footsteps banged down the stairs, pulling Tanner's attention away. Tucker flew past him and out the door. Tanner watched the entire scene with confusion freezing his tongue.

"You're here," Tucker said, sounding ridiculously happy, and doubling Tanner's confusion. They both walked away without as much as a goodbye. Still, Tanner couldn't look away. Tucker tried taking Orion's hand. "We should totally hold hands."

Orion smacked his hand away. "Keep your fucking cooties over there. There's no telling where those hands have been."

Tucker's laughter had Tanner blinking and backing away. He closed the door on the pair, shaking his head. Soon, he would have to find out the story behind that one. It seemed he had missed a lot in the past few months.

Henry appeared in the kitchen door-way, holding his coffee cup, and looking sexy as fuck. "Was that Tucker leaving?"

Tanner nodded.

Henry smirked. "Toby is working and now Tucker is gone too. Sounds like we have the house to ourselves. Whatever shall we do?"

Tanner turned away and headed for the stairs. He knew Henry would follow. His old man had an appetite. Tanner had what he needed, and always would.

Please keep an eye out for the next Cubs for Rent, *Next Best Thing*.

About the Author

CHARITY PARKERSON IS AN award-winning and multi-published author with several companies. Born with no filter from her brain to her mouth, she decided to take this odd quirk and insert it in her characters.

*Eight-time Readers' Favorite Award Winner

*2015 Passionate Plume Award Finalist

*2013 Reviewers' Choice Award Winner

FIRST LOSER

*2012 ARRA Finalist for Favorite Paranormal Romance

*Five-time winner of The Mistress of the Darkpath

Connect with her online:

*Sign up for her newsletter: https://sendfox.com/charityparkerson

*Join her readers' group on Facebook: http://bit.ly/CharitysTribe

*Website: https://www.charityparkerson.com

*A list of her social media accounts and giveaways all in one place: http://hy.page/charityparkerson